THE TRAITORS

THE TRAITORS

Peter Chester

CHIVERS

THORNDIKE

This Large Print book is published by BBC Audiobooks Ltd, Bath, England and by Thorndike Press®, Waterville, Maine, USA.

Published in 2006 in the U.K. by arrangement with the Author.

Published in 2006 in the U.S. by arrangement with Peter Chambers.

U.K. Hardcover ISBN 1–4056–3534–7 (Chivers Large Print)
U.K. Softcover ISBN 1–4056–3535–5 (Camden Large Print)
U.S. Softcover ISBN 0–7862–8146–4 (British Favorites)

The text of this Large Print edition is unabridged.
Other aspects of the book may vary from the original edition.

Set in 16 pt. New Times Roman.

Printed in Great Britain on acid-free paper.

British Library Cataloguing in Publication Data available

Library of Congress Cataloging-in-Publication Data

Chester, Peter, 1924–
        The traitors / by Peter Chester.
                p.   cm.
        "Thorndike Press large print British favorites."—T.p. verso.
        ISBN 0–7862–8146–4 (lg. print : sc : alk. paper)
        1. Americans—England—London—Fiction. 2. London
(England)—Fiction. 3. Large type books. I. Title.
PR6066.H463T73 2005
823'.914—dc22   2005021960

CHAPTER ONE

Ten-fifteen in the morning in late July and already my clothes were sticking to me. It was the sixth day of the heat wave that had taken charge of London and most of southern England, and let me tell you, anybody who says it can't get hot in England hasn't been there at the right time. The hot, dry pavement, unnaturally whitened by the blistering sun, glared up at squinting eyes, and my feet already weighed about half a ton apiece. Two young chicks in matching yellow sun-tops and fresh white linen skirts came towards me, laughing and chattering the way young chicks do in any weather. I didn't spare them a second glance. Now will you believe how hot it was? A policeman stood by a traffic crossing, shirt sleeves rolled up to the elbow, dark patches under his arms and across his back. From where he stood he could just see the water playing from the fountains in Trafalgar Square. Well, that's one way to drive a man mad. I crossed the street to hide in the four-foot strip of shade that hugged the buildings on that side. Eight minutes later I was standing opposite the office waiting for a break in the traffic so I could dash across. Today it was more of a shambling lope than a dash, but I guess the cars and what-have-you must have been feeling the heat too. They certainly weren't after any land-speed records, and I managed to make the other side with only two curses and one waved fist.

After the comparative cool, the heat outside the office seemed especially fierce, but I took time out to admire the layout before going in. I have the whole of the first floor front now. The four-foot red letters told all the world where to find Stevens Personal Service, and underneath were the twelve inch capitals that said 'for visiting U.S. Citizens'. It was a little over a year ago that I got the bright idea which now permitted me to roll up to work at ten-thirty in the am. Every year since the war the European holiday had been a growing favourite back home. Hundreds of thousands of vacationing people from the United States were heading eastwards across the Atlantic with a wallet full of dollars and a few vague thoughts about seeing Big Ben. They wanted accommodation, travel facilities, entertainment, and above all, information. Most of their requirements were of course adequately met by existing organisations, but not for everything at once, all in the same office. A friend of mine once told me he reckoned to spend between one and two hours every single day of his European tour finding out where to go and how to get there. Not because people weren't willing to help him, but because he himself wasn't always sure of what he wanted to do, or where to go to find out. With Europeans that's O.K. The facilities are available, and if you want to use them, there they are. The people know all about it. But the visitor doesn't, and that's where Stevens Personal Service comes in. The visitor makes just one call, and my office does the rest.

For an inclusive charge of ten U.S. dollars, my office will personally service one American family for its entire stay. If they want suggestions, guide books, maps, tour itineraries, information, it all comes out of the same ten bucks. Most of them think so well of the way they're looked after, they get us to do other things, too. Book a theatre, a 'plane ticket, stuff like that, and then there's a small administration charge. We guarantee satisfaction in every detail, and we see the client gets it, right down to the folded newspaper handed over as the train pulls out. Americans appreciate service and are prepared to pay for it. In London they pay me, and if you don't think I'm likely to get fat on just a ten-dollar fee, you haven't talked to my tailor lately.

I went into the building and across to the private lift which I'd had installed for that one-floor ride. The kid in the plum-coloured uniform hopped in, and away we went. Upstairs I stepped out into the entrance hall. An alert young guy, immaculate in a grey business suit, came through a doorway.

'Oh, Mr. Stevens. Good morning.'

'Morning, Jim.'

I nodded and went on through the general office. Here behind their expensive desks sat the people who made the thing tick. The highly paid and hard worked personal couriers. Most of them were too busy to look up, but I got one or two smiles on the way. I have to pass through Pat Richmond's office to get to my own. There was a fat, unpleasant-looking man standing by her desk.

'. . . and I'm not here to deal with hired help. When I say . . .'

'Morning, Pat.'

'Good morning.'

The fat man broke off what he was saying and looked at me. He was wearing a blue suit of some linen material that flapped around him like a sack. His tie was pulled away from the shirt collar, and the shirt hadn't seen a laundry lately. There was a bald patch in the middle of the thin, dark hair, and perspiration stood out on the loose folds of skin that hung slackly on his pasty white face. The eyes were recessed in deep pouches, like those of a fox from cover. He didn't inspire me at all.

'You Stevens?'

The voice added nothing to his charms, and had started its life somewhat less than a thousand miles from Flatbush.

'What can I do for you?'

'This here's the Stevens Personal Service, ain't it? Well, ain't it?'

I nodded.

'That's what it says on the sign.'

'Damn right. So when I come here for service, I want it from Stevens, not some lackey.'

'The people here are highly-trained operators. I'm lucky they work for me. They don't qualify as lackeys, friend.'

When I call anybody friend, I'm getting irritable. Pat jumped in quickly.

'This gentleman insisted on seeing you personally, Mr. Stevens. I explained that you weren't here.'

Good for Pat. She never lets them rile her, and she tries to keep me in line, too, with the awkward ones.

'All right. Well, I'm here now. Come into the office.'

I opened the door and waited while he passed me, then gave Miss Richmond a large wink. She grinned back cheerfully. Somebody had had the sense to open up the windows, but just the same there wasn't enough air in the place to keep a fly healthy. The fat man crossed to the window situated at one side of my desk and looked out. Then he turned back into the room.

'Sure is hot,' he muttered.

I nodded. He pointed to the telephones.

'Those things switched through to

anybody?' he demanded.

I didn't see what business it was of his, but I shook my head from side to side.

'Nope. I have to flick this key over before anybody can hear me.'

The fat man grunted, then removed a large white handkerchief from a pocket and mopped at his face. He could have saved himself the trouble. As he took the handkerchief away, there was a fresh supply of moisture all ready for mopping.

'I never been here before. They told me to pack my woollen underwear when I left the other side.'

'This heat is kind of unusual,' I replied. 'Still, you didn't call in here for a weather forecast, did you, Mr.—?'

'Rourke. Lloyd A. Rourke. No, I didn't. A friend of mine said you were the man to see about my problems.'

'Does your friend have a name I'd know?'

'Maybe.' Rourke lowered the handkerchief and looked carefully into my face. 'The name is Charlie Gray.'

So that was it. I said slowly:

'I know three, four guys named Charlie Gray. Which one are we talking about?'

'Charlie said you'd be sure to remember him because of his uncle.'

'His uncle Sammy?'

'The same.'

I held out my hand and Rourke took it

firmly. Then I said:

'There's a place called "The Milk Jug" in Leicester Square. Big meeting place for tourists to have an early drink. I'll be there at eleven-fifteen.'

'Right.'

I opened the door for him and stood there until he was half way across Pat Richmond's office.

'Don't you worry,' I called out, 'they'll be real good seats.'

He turned and smiled like a baby that's got its own way.

'Not good seats, Stevens. The best in the house. I can pay it,' he crowed, patting himself on the chest.

'You'll be well satisfied. My personal guarantee.'

When the other door had closed behind him, I let the smile dissolve from my face and scowled. Pat looked at me enquiringly.

'Was that all he wanted? Some seats?'

'Yes, Patsy, just seats. How much of a nuisance was he?'

'Oh,' she tilted her nose. It's a nice nose. 'Not as bad as some. But if I'd known the fat idiot only wanted some tickets . . .'

'Now, now, Miss Richmond. We are here to provide what they want. And I guess the man was right. It does say "Stevens Personal Service" out front.'

'Of course.' She picked up a pencil. 'Tell me

what he wants and I'll lay it on.'

I shook my head.

'No dice. He's called me on that "Personal" tag. I'll get the seats and deliver them myself.'

She smiled. Pat Richmond is rising twenty-four, a little over medium height and carrying around one hundred and thirty pounds. The grey eyes are calm mostly, and the ash-blonde hair neatly pushed into whatever some half-male hair artist dictates is the new style. Sitting behind the desk in her immaculate light-weight suit of cool green, Pat was every inch the super-efficient, impersonal personal secretary. She ought to be, considering what I had to pay her. Not that I complain, don't get me wrong, Pat Richmond is the best in the business. I wondered how she could look so cool in that weather, and recalled briefly that one of the staff once said she had ice water in her veins.

'Well, I'll get along and fix up our friend,' I said. 'That guy is a trouble-maker if I ever saw one. If he isn't satisfied, he'll go out of his way to spread the good word all over the United States. I know the type.'

'Will you be back before lunch?' she asked.

'Oh—er—lunch. Maybe, but don't count on it. There's nothing special for me until this afternoon, is there?'

'No.'

A few minutes later I was back out on the street, now thirty minutes hotter than when I left it. The crowds were beginning to thicken up with incoming shoppers and tourists, rubbernecking at the wonderful stuff in the shops. Stuff they could have bought cheaper where they started out from, or is the heat making me just a touch surly? I called in at the Lights Up Theatre Bureau and had a few words with the guy who runs the joint. When I came out, there were two centre stalls in my pocket for the most unget-at-able show in town. I walked around to Leicester Square and sat down under one of those shady trees to take the weight off my feet before getting down to business with Rourke.

Maybe I should have mentioned this before, but anyway here it is. Back in Waldron City, California, before I dreamed up this Stevens Personal Service trick, I was a private investigator. Had a good business, too, plenty of contacts, even stood well with the local law, and that's more than many a P.I. can claim. Then, as I say, I got this idea of mine and decided to give it a whirl. When I was all set to leave Waldron, I had a couple of visitors, all the way from Washington, D.C. They knew all about me, of course, because I'd done a couple of years with Intelligence after the war, while I was still in the Army. I'd also been called in on another little matter for Uncle Sam not long before.

The Washington boys liked the sound of the new venture. They said it ought to do well, and it would suit their book just fine to have somebody like me in London. Somebody with a nice respectable business, and plenty of contacts with a high percentage of American visitors. If I ever heard anything in the ordinary way of business which might interest the Government, they knew they could rely on me to pass it on to the proper source. It would probably never be necessary to call on me for anything, but in case it ever did crop up, how would I feel about going back on to the Reserve, so that my position would be safeguarded from both my own and their point of view? That was the general line of chatter they handed me, and I'm not going to tell you I was particularly hopped up over the idea. But I was assured that they regarded the whole affair as just a little insurance matter. There I'd be, and there I would remain, except for a very occasional special caper that just may occur. I finally bought a ticket and, to do those two boys justice, nobody had asked to see the stub until now—over a year later. Rourke was the first person I'd seen who'd made any reference to it. In fact, it was quite a surprise when he went into that Charlie Gray routine and I'd almost forgotten my lines. Almost. Somehow a thing like that you don't ever properly forget. Anyway, speaking of Rourke, here it was ten minutes after eleven, and time I showed at the 'Milk-Jug'.

I left the pleasant shade with some

reluctance and wandered across to the place. You probably know it, so I won't bother with a description. Any time between eleven in the morning and two-thirty in the afternoon, the place is bulging at the seams with exiles from the U.S.A. Evenings hardly a soul goes near the place, but those morning sessions are really something. Don't ask me why, I've noticed it in other towns, other countries. A place has a certain period during the day which is its busy time, and nothing the management or anybody else can do is going to adjust that period by one minute. So here I was in the 'Milk-Jug', which was already two-thirds filled, and would be jam-packed in another half hour. All around me people were social-ing away in the time-honoured way, waving their dry martinis, Scotch-on-the-rocks, Bourbon and soda, and all the other accessories to chit-chat.

A gangling Georgian was arguing with a sharp-featured Connecticut man. I edged past a group from Minnesota who were trying to explain to an elderly pair of Philadelphians why it was important to go to Stratford-on-Avon early in the morning. I wished I'd had time to catch some more of that. Why should it be important? Anyway, there was the man I'd come to see, hunched against the wall with a tall glass in his hand, beads of moisture trickling down the outside to show how cold the drink was. He waved and I nodded. At the bar I stopped long enough to wrap my hand around another cold glass with a measure of good Scotch whisky inside it.

'Hey there, Stevens.' Rourke beckoned me over. 'How about those tickets of mine?'

I grinned widely.

'You bet,' I replied. 'All fixed up.'

This brilliant exchange had served to get me across to Rourke, and explain to any interested party who had half an ear just what our business was. It's an odd thing, the way you can hold the most private discussions in public if the place is crowded and noisy enough. I sat down next to Rourke with my back rested on the wall, and took a sip at the drink.

'What gives?' I said, keeping my voice down, but not low enough to be obvious. Nobody seemed interested in us anyway, not that that meant anything at all.

'I'm told you haven't done much in our line lately.' Rourke made it a statement.

'That's about right. I didn't ride a bicycle lately either, but I'll give you a quarter mile start in a mile race. You never forget how to ride a bicycle.'

He nodded thoughtfully, and spent a while studying a young couple who were new arrivals. Then he said:

'You don't forget how to ride a bicycle, but after a long lay-off you don't enter for a championship race either. You have to pedal your way back into shape first.'

'All right. Am I supposed to be entering a race?'

He nodded again. I found myself wishing he'd look at me once in a while. Now he was studying a broad-shouldered, swarthy character who was proudly explaining all about his camera to another guy who seemed to wish he'd never come into the place.

'This here's a championship race. For the championship of the world.' He did look at me then, and his eyes were hard. 'Right now I've got the ball and I'll tell you this, I'm not going to pass it to somebody who isn't in any shape to handle it.'

I tried to tell myself I wasn't getting mad with this fat man. I said reasonably:

'Look, Rourke, I didn't come looking for you. You came to me. Reason you came is because you were sent. What's this pitch about a ball?'

'Don't get sore, Stevens. I told the family I didn't think you were right for this. They said to take a look at you, talk to you. If I didn't think you'd do, you were out. That's all.'

'I see. Well, now you see me. What don't you like?'

He considered.

'It's not as simple as that. What worries me is this twelve months you been loafing around over here, getting people tickets and stuff. You must be rusty.'

'The tickets and stuff seemed like a pretty

13

good scheme to the family when we talked about it. Build it up, they said, concentrate on the cover. Now I'm so goddamned covered, the family can't see me. 'Listen to this.' I hurried on as he started to interrupt. 'Things aren't always as quiet as you may think around my organisation.'

'Such as—?' he said.

'Such as last November. There was a stabbing incident in Turin. Man severely wounded, hospitalised for two months. Some people were of a mind to put the arm on the young son of a prominent U.S. industrialist who was visiting at the time. The kid was a little wild, and if he'd caused any trouble, it might have upset some rather delicate import-export deals his father was negotiating. Luckily it was proved that the kid had left Turin for London the day before the incident. Stevens Personal Service took care of that one.'

I told him a couple of other little things that the 'Service' had handled, things a little remote from setting up tour itineraries. He didn't interrupt once. In fact it was hard to be sure he was even listening. His eyes roamed around the 'Milk-Jug' all the time, like those of any other guy who'd come in out of the heat for a drink. When I got through he said:

'How far is the nearest park?'

'Five minutes in a cab.'

'Get one. Wait across the street. I'll be over in two minutes.'

14

I got up, said something or other, laughed and clapped him on the back. He grinned up at me. Then I emptied the glass, stood it on a table nearby and walked out. There was a cab-stand nearby. I got in the first one and we rolled away, to a spot fifty yards away from the entrance to the 'Milk-Jug', and on the far side of the street. As we got there the bulky figure of Rourke appeared, threading his way through the traffic. I opened the door and he got in. We said nothing until we reached Green Park. I tapped on the glass and the driver pulled up. Then we were in the Park. Plenty of people were around, mostly taking life easy. On the baked grass, kids were fooling around with balls of all shapes and sizes. The heat didn't seem to worry them at all. They rushed around, kicking and yelling.

'There's a seat,' said Rourke, pointing.

It was exactly right for the job. There wasn't a scrap of shade within fifty yards of that wooden bench. Nobody else was likely to join us. We sat down and Rourke passed cigarettes.

'I think you'll do,' he said.

It wasn't a personal thing. In Rourke's business, and mine now again, you don't have any personal opinions or feelings. You consider evidence, facts, weigh them and decide. It's not easy at times, especially with people, but there's no personal element involved. The only issue of importance is the caper. Just the same, I'm not pretending I wasn't glad to hear Rourke say what he did. None of us likes to think he's no longer the man he was. I smoked my cigarette and waited.

'I guess you know Ed Masters is coming over here?' enquired Rourke.

'Sure. I read something about it. Tomorrow, isn't it?'

'M'm. Let me put you in the picture about Masters. You've read pieces about him and what he's been up to back home, but I want to be sure you understand this thing.'

I nodded. Senator Edward P. Masters had been getting a little space in the British newspapers as an anti-Communist. There was some reportage about his activities, but you can never tell from occasional clippings where a man like Masters fits into the general scene, what his real significance is on his own ground. I was about to find out.

'Masters is just about the most prominent figure in the anti-Red scene nowadays. It isn't just a question of a few speeches, an odd committee or two. Masters is conducting an all-out, twenty-four-hours-a-day campaign. He's just about the hottest propaganda we've got. And,' Rourke heaved a large sigh, 'like most of these characters, he's hard to handle. Never a week goes by but he sets Washington by the ears with some new play. It's been said you can't walk a hundred yards in the Capitol without passing five guys whose ears are burning on account of Ed Masters.'

I could tell by Rourke's tone that he'd had some experience of all this himself.

'And giving the family plenty of headaches, too, huh?'

'Right. The guy means well, but he demonstrates the big fault with a genuine democracy. That is this. While there's such a thing as diplomacy in the world, the Government can't explain every solitary action it takes to every farmer's boy who likes to ask. Now and then you have to pull the blanket over, and that Masters, he hates blankets. Anyway,' he turned to me, 'Ed Masters is now coming to Europe. Says he's not satisfied that the older democracies are taking a firm enough line with the Reds. He's going to take a personal look-see.'

'I see. Ought to make old Uncle Sammy a lot of friends this side.'

Rourke sighed.

'Yeah. He's staying four days. If he's in good shape, and he always is in good shape, he ought to set back our relationship with the boys over here about two years. Still,' he straightened up on the seat and mopped at his face with a handkerchief, 'that part of it is not your worry. Your job, compared to that of the boys in the striped pants, is a cake-walk.'

'I'm glad to hear it.'

He grunted.

'There's been a little buzz. It won't be any

17

news to you that there are some countries, less than a million miles from London, who don't have a very high opinion of the Senator. It would be very nice if something happened to him while he was here. Something fatal for preference.'

'Why here especially?' I asked. 'Seems to me there'd be plenty of chances to knock him off in the States. Plenty of people on hand for that kind of work, too.'

'Yeah. But this is not just some gang fight, or an insurance killing. This is big political headlines. The guy rates with John Doe as the all-American anti-Red. If he got killed at a rally in New York or somewhere, the wave of public feeling would be phenomenal, and all directed against a certain quarter. That might not suit the people in that quarter particularly well. But,' he pointed at me with a fat and stubby forefinger, 'if he buys it on this side, not all the feelings will be anti-Red. There'll be plenty of people around to point out Masters was criticising the Old World. Plenty of people to quote odd cuts from speeches which are anti-Europe. And, in the last resort, the fact would remain that the guy was killed here. Not properly protected, insufficient vigilance from the police and so forth. There are always plenty of guys ready to knock Europe, for a million different reasons, and they'd all be up on their hind legs before the sound of the shooting died away.'

It made sense. Senator Masters was getting to be a big headache to certain foreign powers. Big enough that something drastic had to be done about him. And here was the chance to do it, and cause some hard feelings between the Western Powers at the same time. I still didn't see where I could help.

'O.K. You've sold me so far. When's my entrance?'

'I'm coming to that. Now, like I said, we've heard this buzz. We would have taken precautions over the man anyway, but now we're sewing the deal up tight. Everybody's in. The diplomats, the F.B.I., Scotland Yard, the British Intelligence, not forgetting the family.'

The family, you'll have gathered, is the way we refer to our own organisation whose precise identity I don't propose to tell you.

'It sounds to me as if anybody who tries to get near the Senator without a dozen passes is going to get severe lead poisoning before they land in the same building with him.'

'I hope you're right. I never say a thing is buttoned up, because I've seen too many capers come undone, but this I will say. If anybody can get to knock off the Senator on his official tour, I'd like to shake them by the hand, because it'll be something outside my experience.'

Rourke began to pick at a thumbnail with a match.

'Now it gets tricky. All these precautions

19

sound good, dammit they are good, but there's one thing that can make monkeys out of the whole bunch of us. That one thing is Senator Edward P. Masters. Let me tell you about Masters. He's a Plain John. Loves to go around being folks with everybody. A mixer, a you're-as-good-as-me character. I don't think I've seen two pictures of him where his suspenders weren't on view. Makes a lot of friends that way. He's a guy everybody knows, a guy who likes a stag party, a poker session, man who's not afraid to take a little drink. You get the picture?'

I nodded.

'These official tours now. They're all right for the public figure, the Senator. But old Ed Masters, he wants to meet ordinary people, get into a pub, a dog-track, maybe even a girlie-show.'

'Got it. Masters ducks the bloodhounds and heads for the ball game, and that's where I come in.'

'Right. Now we know he's going to do this. He's even been offered a schedule which includes time off for that kind of thing, and we'd know where he was doing it. But he doesn't trust anything that's organised for him. And he'll tell you that the Government service is riddled with pimps and commies anyway. Does that have a familiar ring?'

It did. I've heard the same sickening claptrap from people who ought to know better, and I'd have expected nothing else from a guy like Masters.

'O.K., here's the pay-off. We've managed to drop a secret word in his ear that the only place in London where he can get the real low-down on what gives, is an outfit run by an American. Place called the Stevens Personal Service. So now you begin to get it.'

He told me the rest. It was practically certain that Masters would get in touch with me soon after arrival. He'd be looking for a little excitement that wasn't on the agenda, and I was to provide it. There was a telephone number on the Grosvenor Exchange and I was to keep this number posted on every move Masters was to make. I was to accompany him personally, although the real protection would be provided by others. That way the family could keep tabs on the great man twenty-four hours in every day. But my cover was to remain. I wasn't to identify myself to anybody, ever, and my code name was 'Jeremy'. My importance to the caper lay in the fact that only Rourke knew who or what I was, and nothing would be permitted to jeopardise my cover.

We sat there maybe half an hour longer while I asked every question I could think of. The Grosvenor number was to be on a round-the-clock schedule so I could report any time. Finally we'd talked it out. We rose, stretched our legs and grinned at each other.

'So I'm back to work at last,' I remarked, unnecessarily.

'Seems likely.'

'Do I get any more instructions? I presume they'll have to come from you, seeing that nobody else knows me?'

Rourke shook his head slowly.

'No more instructions. Next that happens is when Masters or that front man of his, Raymond Bentley, gets in touch with you. You won't be seeing me any more.'

Great. It was comforting to know the family hadn't changed at all. Here's a gun, don't get killed, but in case you do, we don't know you.

'But look, Rourke—'

He'd been about to leave. Now he paused and half-turned back, waiting. I said:

'Suppose there's a hitch? Suppose I get in a jam?'

The fat man's face was hard. A trickle of perspiration ran down the side of his nose while he looked at me cheerfully.

'Don't,' he said, and walked away.

CHAPTER TWO

I gave the office a miss even earlier than usual that afternoon. It was a little after three when I closed my door behind me.

'I'm not feeling so great, Pat,' I announced.

'Think I'll knock off and go home.'

She was all concern.

'I am sorry. Nothing very serious, I hope?'

'Oh, no. Probably just a little too much of your London fog.'

I waved a weary arm towards the window, where a brilliant shaft of sunlight, slanted its way to the floor. La Richmond grinned.

'I'll try not to disturb you. Will you be staying at home?'

'Yeah. And don't worry about disturbing me. I'm not sick, you know. Anybody wants to talk to me personally, give 'em my home number in the usual way. You know the rules. Nothing is too much trouble for the customers.'

'Yes, sir.' She gave me an unmilitary salute.

The cover was working. Already I was preparing the way, thinking ahead, considering alternatives, weighing up. That's why I left early. It gave me a chance to tell Pat Richmond I'd be home all evening, without giving her reason to wonder why I'd want her to know. I wanted her to know so that she'd be sure to tell callers where to find me. Ordinarily I wouldn't have mentioned these things, so I had to leave early feeling a little low. Don't I trust Pat Richmond? That has nothing to do with it. There was a caper on, and under those circumstances you cover, backtrack, check and then recover. Sure it's elaborate, sure it's a lot of unnecessary effort. Sure most of the work is

23

wasted. So why bother? Because I've been trained to bother, and the result of all the training and the bother is that I'm thirty-four years old and alive. In this business you come up against all kinds of guys, but when you meet one over thirty, and that's not so often, you can be sure he was one of the ones who was listening while teacher was talking.

I have an apartment in one of those squares you hear so much about. It's a comfortable place, with everything now arranged the way I like it. The apartment covers the whole of the second floor, and from the front windows you can look down into a little railed-off park. The park gate is locked, but the regular residents have keys and can stroll around in there whenever they want. Mostly it's a spot for children and nursemaids, and somewhere for the older people to sit and take it easy. Somebody once told me that square has hardly changed in a hundred and fifty years, and it's easy to believe. If you happened to look out and see a carriage pull up, with guys wearing powdered wigs, you wouldn't feel it was out of place. That's my square, and that's the way I like it, and that's why I won't give the address. Let's just say I live at No. 86, Quiet Square, when I'm home. Right now I was home and liking it. One of the habits I've picked up from the British is the one where you sit and stare at a crossword puzzle in a newspaper for maybe two hours before throwing the thing in the ash-can. I was puzzling about whose chariot it was that burned bright like flame when the 'phone clattered. According to my watch it was six-forty. A man's voice said:

'Mr. Stevens?'

'Uh-huh.'

'My name is Bentley, Raymond Bentley.'

I didn't know how Bentley could be calling. He was Masters' front-man, official title, personal secretary, and Masters wasn't due until the next day, Wednesday. Also, I wasn't necessarily supposed to know who Bentley was.

'What can I do for you, Mr. Bentley?'

'I'd like to see you, if it can be arranged. I'd like to avail myself of the services of your organisation.'

His voice was of that clipped New England variety. Mr. Bentley was a product of an institution which has provided a good proportion of our administrators in one field or another.

'Well, I don't know, Mr. Bentley. This is my home number you've called. The people at my office should be able to provide whatever service you require. Shall I give you the number?'

'I've already called your office. I really would prefer to see you personally. You would find our conversation interesting, I think I may say.'

I pretended to think about it.

'Well, O.K., if you think so. Never turn away business, that's me.'

I laughed my business laugh, and he replied with his polite laugh. Then I told him the address and he said he'd be around soon after seven. That didn't give me a lot of time. I dialled the Grosvenor number. On the second ring, the receiver was lifted at the other end. There was a second sound I couldn't quite identify, but I was sure the conversation was either going to be recorded or tapped on another extension. Nobody spoke, so I said:

'This is Jeremy.'

'Go ahead, Jeremy. Charlie Gray here.'

'Raymond Bentley just called me. He's coming to see me at seven o'clock.'

'Very well. Report conversation when possible.'

And I was holding a dead 'phone.

'Thanks for all the interest,' I muttered, replacing it.

I wondered if I could risk watching for Bentley's arrival from the window. It would help me to know whether he had a car, for instance, and whether there was anyone else in it. I decided against looking out in case anyone was watching. After all, it was only a business call so far as I knew. Why should I care how he got there?

The door bell sounded at five minutes after seven. I opened it and found myself looking at a man about five-nine and slim. Despite the heat, Mr. Raymond Bentley was dressed in a dark cloth suit, immaculate white shirt complete with half-inch cuff projections, and a striped tie. He even carried a black Homburg.

'Mr. Bentley? Come on in.'

'Thank you.'

He left the hat on a small table by the door and I led him inside.

'Kind of hot,' I offered. 'How 'bout a drink? I do have ice.'

'Thanks. Do you have any beer?'

I had beer. I had half a refrigerator filled with frosted cans. I broke out a couple and got us sitting down near the open window.

'On a vacation, Mr. Bentley?'

'Not exactly. A business trip would be nearer to the mark.'

He was dark. Smooth black hair kept firmly in place with brilliantine, dark eyes set against finely-modelled features. There was nothing about Mr. Bentley to suggest that he'd come up the hard way. Or any other way, by my guess. Mr. Bentley was already up when he was born. He attacked the beer with quick, neat movements. Neat, that's it. He was neat all over.

'Mr. Stevens, I have been given to understand, by people whose opinions I respect, that you are a man of discretion.'

'I would hope so. Why, my business wouldn't last a week if I didn't know how to mind my own affairs. What are you getting at?'

'Do you know who I am?' He answered the question with a question.

I pretended to think about it.

'No, I don't think—Bentley.' I screwed up my face, then smiled my honest smile. 'No. Beats me. Hope it doesn't give offence?'

He shook his head.

'Not in the least. You may have got the answer if you'd been living in the States recently. I am the personal secretary of a prominent politician. Senator Edward P. Masters.'

'Masters? The big Anti-Commie man? Well, what d'you know!'

'Senator Masters, as you probably are aware, arrives in this country tomorrow on a visit.'

'That's right. I read something about it,' I nodded importantly. 'I like to keep up to date on U.S. visitors. My business, you know.'

'Quite so.' He finished his beer. 'I have arrived ahead of the Senator so that I may inspect the arrangements for his visit. See that everything is in order, you understand.'

I understood.

'Now, Mr. Stevens, you will be aware of the type of programme the Senator will have to fill. Speeches, banquets, press interviews, and so forth. I can tell you from experience, these lightning tours are exhausting. Very exhausting.'

Sympathetic clucking from my corner.

'So you see, the Senator will have virtually no rest from the official round.'

'They must leave him some time for sleeping, I guess?'

'Ah, yes. But that is never enough, believe me. The harrowing part about these tours is the sameness of it all. What one needs,' he looked at me sharply, 'is not sleep. It's relaxation, a complete change.'

I wagged my head, to show I was with it.

'Makes sense. You mean a real break, something different.'

'Yes.'

I weighed up what he'd said, then:

'But surely, the boys in Washington, or wherever they plan these tours, they know all this? Don't they make any allowance for it?'

Bentley passed cigarettes and we got them going. Then he sat back deep in his chair. He was one of those guys who always look right. If it had been me in that chair, it would have taken a good man to be sure I wasn't a sack of potatoes, but Bentley merely looked relaxed, and somehow—well, here's that word again—neat. Through a cloud of smoke he said:

'That's precisely the difficult part. You see, Senator Masters is not without his enemies. There's even been a suggestion that someone may make an attempt on his life while he's over here.'

He paused so I'd get the full effect of that. Some contribution from me was evidently in

29

order.

'Here? In England? Nah.' I flapped a disbelieving hand. 'Not in a hundred years.'

'I realise it doesn't sound feasible. But just the same, Mr. Stevens, I assure you the suggestion I mentioned came from a well-informed source.'

It convinced me. I made one of those whistling noises, down-scale.

'Well, well. Even here, eh? Go ahead, Mr. Bentley. Tell me the rest.'

'As I was saying, Washington has heard of this, and as a result, very extensive security measures are being taken in respect of the Senator's visit. One result of this is that the so-called relaxation periods in his itinerary are not altogether satisfactory.'

'I think I get it. They expect him to go into a bar with G-men holding guns on all the customers. And the Senator doesn't expect to get a lot of fun that way.'

Bentley uncrossed his legs and leaned towards me.

'Your example is a little—er—extreme, but the picture is not so inaccurate as I would like. My chief is supposed to relax in surroundings which have been sterilised.'

'Sort of whooping it up in a dentist's waiting-room, eh?'

A pained look crossed his face before he could stop it. Mr. Raymond Bentley was evidently finding it difficult to approve of my

30

style of delivery. Nevertheless, he got himself in hand.

'As you say. Now here is what the Senator wants. He wants to slip away from the routine, just once or twice, and see a little of the lighter side of London. He has been told that you're the man to help him. Are you?'

I picked up my beer-can. It was empty, so I did the next best thing with it, and held its gleaming coldness against my forehead. Great sensation.

'Easiest thing in the world to arrange—but,' I said, as a satisfied smile appeared on Bentley's face, 'I don't know that I think much of the idea.'

The smile disappeared.

'May one ask why?'

'Sure.' I rolled the can over to the other side of my head. 'I've been listening to what you've told me. According to you, Edward P. Masters could be in danger on this side. The security boys want to keep him alive, so they sit on his tail all the time. He wants to jump school and you want me to help. Have you thought that if there's really anybody after him, we will be providing them with a perfect opportunity to knock him off? No guards, no guns, just a sitting Senator. I'm thinking about how I'd feel if that happened. How would you feel, Bentley?'

He stood up from the chair, rubbing his hands together nervously.

'What you say is true.' He picked up an ornament and set it carefully back in place. 'I'd better tell you something else.'

'Might be a thought,' I answered.

'When the chief came out with this crazy scheme—all right . . .' He saw I was about to interrupt . . . 'I know it's crazy—I told him pretty much the same things you've told me. He'd got your name from somewhere. I was against it, against you for that matter. You don't know him yet, but let me tell you, Ed Masters is not the man to be told what he can and can't do. He gave me the choice of fixing up with you on his behalf, or he'd just wander away on his own and find some fun. In the first case I'd know where he was at least and there'd be two people with him, you and I. In the second case he'd be entirely alone, with no chance of protection. You can see he didn't give me a lot of choice. That's why I'm here and that's the whole story.'

'Oh.'

In his precise and well-mannered way, Bentley was practically on his knees to me. I almost felt sorry for the guy. I said:

'And now you're putting me on the same spot. I can either do what you want, or just sit around here till I read in the papers about the mysterious disappearance or death of the prominent U.S. statesman, Senator Edward P. Masters?'

'That about sizes it up, Stevens.'

He waited while I thought about it. I let him wait a while so I wouldn't look too eager.

'Looks like I'm really over a barrel, doesn't it?'

We grinned at each other resignedly.

'I'm very relieved. Masters is a difficult man at times, but I believe he has a great future. That's why I stay with him, and that's why I'm going to keep him alive if I can.'

'Well, if I'm in, I'm in. Why don't you sit down, relax, have another beer and tell me a few little things about the guy?'

He did, and for an hour or so kept me listening hard while he sketched in a picture of Masters. Mostly it fitted with what I already knew, both from the press and Rourke. This business of slipping away from the limelight didn't seem to be quite as harmless as Rourke had imagined. What Masters seemed to be looking for at these times was not merely a chance to enjoy himself without publicity. It was more of an opportunity for the kind of enjoyment that wouldn't stand publicity, quite a different thing. Not that Bentley gave much away, don't get me wrong, but by asking the right questions and listening hard for the bits of the answers that were left out, I was able to form a shrewd idea of what passed for fun with the Senator. It didn't help to make me love him any.

Bentley was a different matter. Somehow I got an impression of a man with a tradition of service behind him. Important service. We don't go in much for a lot of kow-towing where I come from, but just the same, we do breed some people who in any less enlightened country would form an aristocracy. Bentley was a typical product of that community, and I always feel a kind of pleasure that people like him come from the same country as people like me. It fitted, too, that he would be doing what he was, working a sixteen-hour day for another guy who was opposed to everything un-American. The Masters would come and go, but the Bentleys would always be around, formal, correct, urbane, tireless. I probably learned nearly as much about Bentley as I did about his boss. Finally it came time for him to leave.

'So what time does the balloon go up tomorrow?' I asked.

'Eleven a.m. the 'plane is due. From then we've got a packed programme till eleven p.m. Exactly twelve hours.'

'Well, I guess that lets me out till Thursday, uh?'

He shook his head decisively.

'If you knew the Senator, you wouldn't have said that. He'll be expecting you tomorrow night, eleven-fifteen. Just for a chat. We'll get down to a few details then about what London has to offer.'

'I can tell you that now. Everything you can get in any other capital city in the world. And better than many of 'em', I replied.

'Well, we won't discuss it now. See you at the hotel to-morrow night.'

We shook hands at the door, and he left. It was ten minutes before nine. I went back and helped myself to some Scotch over ice, and thought about my visitor. At nine I picked up the telephone and did my song and dance for the Grosvenor number. I got the same encouraging replies, grunts and hisses mainly. Then the cold impersonal voice at the other end said:

'Okay, Jeremy. Report tomorrow night's meeting at first opportunity.'

And that was that.

There wasn't too much daylight around now, though the sky was an unnaturally bright blue considering the hour. I stood at the window looking down into the square. It's a favourite habit of mine in the evening. A laugh drifted on the still air, and a guy was holding open the door of one of those low-on-the-road automobiles, while a girl stood on the sidewalk arguing with him. They seemed a nice young couple to me, and the argument couldn't have been very serious, because the boy in the tweeds suddenly got tired of it, picked up the girl and dumped her in the car. That raised a protesting laugh. Then he jumped clean over her into the driver's seat and they were off. I grinned and moved over to watch their progress. Something made me look back to where they'd started from. There was a man standing close to the park railings. Despite the heat, he was wearing a buttoned-up raincoat and a slouch hat and he was looking at me. When he realised he'd been spotted, he turned away and paced slowly along the side of the park, away from me. I had something to think about as I moved back into the room.

The guy downstairs standing by the railings was an unknown quantity. He could be a member of the family. The family sometimes keeps tabs on its own. The opposition may have sent him along to check on whoever Bentley went to visit. The British police or I-men could have sent him on that same errand. Come to think of it, he could be just a guy who happened to be downstairs standing by the railings, but I didn't think so. I'm a simple-minded sort of man. If I'm mixed up in anything and people start looking interested in me, I don't ever imagine it's because they admire my baby-blue eyes. My eyes are grey anyway. The best thing to do about the man in the slouch hat was forget him, and I decided to do just that. Whoever he was rooting for, he had me spotted, and the only alternatives were either to let him know he'd been seen, thus tipping him off that I may be expecting something of the kind, or else go into my routine about what an open book my life was and what a plain legit. character I was. All of which meant I didn't have any alternative at all.

Different people have different reactions, and what gives with you, I don't know, but with me, comes nine of a hot July evening, and I get to thinking about taking the air. Especially the air around one or two cool bars I could name, and if there chances to be maybe a cool blonde or two in the vicinity, I don't complain too loud.

I took a shower, heaving all my linen into the basket first. Now that the sun had disappeared in favour of the moon shift, I could really appreciate that water. The fresh shirt I picked out had a feeling of luxury about it. As I flipped the grey woollen tie round my neck, I thought briefly of the dame who'd given it to me. She had been a stenographer from K.C. who'd saved up two years for the trip over here. Her itinerary was spaced out generously to cover fourteen European countries in four weeks. She told me she was going to live it up to the full, the whole trip, and I had to admit that her three days in England gave me to understand she meant it. Her idea was that I should personally conduct this tour, but after three days I had to cry quits. Maybe I'm not as young as I was.

One of the few disadvantages of my present address was that I had to garage my car in a place on the corner of the square, maybe two hundred yards from where I live, which doesn't sound far until you've walked it in a storm with no coat. I didn't look around for you-know-who. So far as I was concerned, there was no reason why an ordinary business character like me should be followed. As I backed the car out on to the road, I did manage to search the street behind with the aid of the driving mirror. There was nobody in sight, but I'd expected that. At least it was flattering, they hadn't sent a beginner to take a look at me. First stop was the Bamboo Hut, an upholstered railway carriage with a liquor licence and twelve cane chairs. I could see no harm in taking a little relaxation. After all, the business I was on wasn't due to start till the evening of the next day, Wednesday. The Bamboo Hut was busy, and it was a struggle to get up to the operations H.Q.

'A long one, Mr. Stevens?'

'A long one, Charlie.'

While he busied around with a pair of silver tongs, picking up ice-cubes and dropping them into the glass, I took a peek at the rest of the customers. There was one guy I knew by sight, the rest were strangers, and that's how I like it. When I'm drinking for business reasons there's plenty places I can go and see people I know. When the drinking is for pleasure, I have a different list of calls. This particular drink Charlie handed over was a real pleasure. I broke out some cigarettes and lit one. All around me people were talking, laughing, a dozen conversations at one time. None of them cared about me, and the feeling was mutual. I got to thinking life could be pleasant on a hot summer evening when a man doesn't have to worry about the rent, and can afford to take aboard some company from a bottle. On the second drink I began to think about other things, other kinds of company the bottle couldn't provide. Neither, as I knew from experience, could the Bamboo Hut. Charlie was between customers and lurking not far from my stool.

'Feel lucky tonight, Charlie?'

He looked at me thoughtfully. Charlie is a short, square man of around fifty. I'd been a regular customer since arriving in England, and there was this game we play sometimes.

'P'raps,' he said. 'How much you got?'

I dived a hand into my pants' pocket and brought out all the silver and copper coins, which I dumped on the counter. Solemnly we took a count.

'Make it eight-and-fivepence?' he queried.

I nodded.

'I'll try you. Two questions I get?'

'Two.'

The game is very simple. We always bet the amount of loose change there was in my pocket at the time. Charlie had to guess where I was headed when I left the Bamboo Hut. The only rule was that it had to be one of the dozen or so places we'd agreed on when we started playing. Charlie hardly ever lost. Now he picked up a snowy-white cloth and began polishing idly at a brandy glass.

'Very smart tonight, Mr. Stevens. You haven't been left home long. I think this is your first call.'

I said nothing, but already I suspected I'd seen the last of my small change.

'Grand evening outside. Makes me feel gay meself. Nice smart clothes. Fair amount of money with you, when you paid for your drink. Car outside.'

He knew that because I'd pulled out my ignition-key at the same time as the change.

'First question. Have you arranged to meet a lady?'

I shook my head.

'Uh, uh.'

He set the glass carefully on the shelf behind him then turned back to me.

'Would you say it was fair, Mr. Stevens, if I saved my other question as a sort of reserve against some future game when I'm finding it a bit difficult?'

'You mean you don't even need it, now?'

'No,' he smiled broadly.

'All right, you shark. With the condition that if you guess wrong, you lose the reserve question.'

'Fair enough.'

Charlie began picking up my money and dropping it in the open drawer of the till. I watched without comment. Then he slammed the drawer and the small bell pinged. A ticket reading 'No Sale' shot into view.

'The Crinoline,' he announced.

And, of course, the Crinoline it was. I had some trouble finding a space to park. There was a guy outside dressed up as an attendant and his contribution to my problem was to regard me with disapproval while I backed and turned and swivelled to get the heap properly settled. As I passed him on my way to the entrance, I said:

'Thanks.'

It couldn't have come out the way I'd meant it to, because all he said was:

'Not at all, sir.'

The management of the Crinoline go out of their way to let you know what a hell of an exclusive place it is, and how lucky you are to be a member. They make a lot of fuss about inspecting the records before letting you in, and I guess it does have some effect on the one-visit-in-six-months members. Makes them feel the trip in from Twickenham was well worth it, just to be privileged to mingle in such company. All I know is that I first went there with another guy and the search of the members' register only proved that we didn't belong, which we already knew. The oily little man who called himself the secretary was prepared to make a special registration seeing that we were American visitors. What that amounted to was each of us giving the greaseball two one-pound notes, and we were in. Nowadays, they knew me, and I walked straight past the desk, down the wide hallway and turned into the largest of the three bars.

She was sitting at a small glass table, and although it turned out there were quite a few other people around, she was the one I saw. Perched on one of the tall stools at the pink counter, I inspected her in the mirror facing me. She was brunette, the hair caught in those small curls to either side of a centre parting. Her face was small and finely chiselled. At the moment the effect was marred by a dissatisfied set to the mouth, and a tempting red mouth such as hers had no business looking that way. She wore a vivid green gown with a halter neck, and I took careful note of the rich cream of her arms and throat. It's not always easy to be sure when they're sitting down, but my money said her figure would match up to her face, and that put her in category 'A'. The bartender made a show of not waiting for me to get through looking so he could serve me. I ordered a Scotch and when he brought it I said:

'The lady in green. I don't think I've seen her here before.'

He looked across without much interest.

'I really couldn't say, sir,' he replied in a low voice. 'So many ladies come in every day. I'm afraid I couldn't be sure.'

For a moment I was inclined not to believe

him, then I reasoned with myself. The man was clocking sixty, and he'd been in this business his whole life. To him the world was a small place filled with used glasses, cigarette butts and aching feet. Maybe he really wouldn't notice any more. I hoped I never got to feeling that way.

'What does she drink?' I asked.

'Dry martini. Doubles. That's her third.'

It wasn't a criticism, not even a comment. Just a plain statement of fact. To me it was interesting. A lady who is waiting for somebody doesn't have time to drink three doubles. Not unless she's been stood up. And a lady who isn't waiting for somebody oughtn't to be left to drink alone. In the big bad city a lady who goes into a place like the Crinoline alone has to take her chances. Chances like me. I slid off the stool, glass in hand, and went across to where she was sitting. There was a fair crowd in the place, but not enough for it to be necessary for me to take the other chair at the small table. I took the other chair at the small table. Her black purse lay in front of me. She picked it up and moved it to her own side, but didn't make a great show of ignoring me. I felt encouraged.

'If you're waiting for someone, I'll be glad to move when he shows,' I said.

She looked at me thoughtfully for a moment before replying. Her voice was rich and deep.

'Are you trying to pick me up?'

It was by no means what I'd expected, but I wasn't going to let her throw me.

'Yes,' I answered. 'I guess I am.'

She smiled quietly, as at some private joke, something I didn't fit in. Then she picked up her glass, drank some of the martini, which I could see was very dry indeed, and set the glass carefully back on the table.

'Good. Consider me picked up. What's your name?'

It was all wrong. She wasn't the usual run of bar pick-ups, and everything about her gave the lie to what she was doing. Well, maybe not everything. After all, she was doing it, when you boil it right down.

'Stevens, Scott Stevens.'

'Mine is Roxanne Baxter.'

I went and got some more drinks. While they were being poured I watched her in the mirror. Her private worries, whatever they were, had been packed away for the night. She had a look at me once or twice, and I tried not to slouch too much. When I got back she said:

'It's rather amusing. I came out with the express intention of getting myself picked up, but I really could not bring myself to endure the types that have tried so far. The more I sat here, the more I began to think I was doing the wrong thing. You came just in time.'

'Lucky me,' I said. 'Tell me, it's probably none of my business, but suppose you'd given up the idea. Were you going to try somewhere else?'

She laughed, and the even white teeth appeared behind those red lips.

'Oh, no. I'd have gone straight home and gone to bed.'

'And where's home?' I prompted.

'Oh, uh.' She shook her head negatively. 'That really is none of your business.'

'O.K.'

So we talked. We talked about everything and nothing and I began to get very glad it was a hot July evening and I'd come to the Crinoline. She was amusing and intelligent, and the thought occurred to me that if very many like Roxanne started banging around bars, it would give business a shot in the arm. On the subject of herself, she was reticent, but I didn't push too hard. There was little doubt in my mind that this girl was married to some character in a high income bracket, and they'd had a fight and here she was out looking for some fun. Mind you, that's only what I thought, and if it were correct, I didn't want it confirmed. I have one of those flexible moral codes which permits me to act the way I was acting so long as I don't actually know anything is wrong. Her eyes were brighter now, and I was beginning to sense her excitement. This could be my lucky evening. Counting the three she'd had before my arrival, and the two since, Roxanne was near the bottom of her fifth helping of double dry martinis. I said:

'On the one hand, I ought to ask if you'd like another drink. On the other hand, I ought to point out that you've already had several, and ask whether you think it's a good idea to have any more.'

She smiled, in a lazy way.

'What's your opinion? A couple more of these and I might get slightly drunk.'

I shook my head.

'Not this man, nothing crude like that. I want you to know exactly what you're doing.'

Leaning across the narrow table she rested her fingers on my hand. She was very close to me, and her lips were slightly parted.

'I know what I'm doing.'

I waited in the carpeted hallway while Roxanne disappeared on one of those errands women always disappear on while guys wait in carpeted hallways. She kept me out there exactly the right length of time, then reappeared, taking my arm and leaning slightly against me. Outside a light breeze was cooling off the scorched pavements. The sky was a deep black and the stars glittered. It was the kind of sky astronomers pray for, and to me it suggested that tomorrow would be as hot as today. I led Roxanne towards the car, helped her into the passenger seat, then walked round the back to get to the other door.

There were two of them, about medium size, and they came at me damned fast with their hands raised. There was a faint whistling sound. I ducked my head, and something thudded across my left shoulder, followed by a second blow which crashed just below my neck. If I hadn't ducked so quickly, those two hits would have made it good night for Stevens. Both the thugs were slightly off-balance with their follow through. I stumbled clear of the car to get more room. Not that I had much hope. I could scarcely move my left hand, and these characters evidently knew their business. The nearest one came at me again in a lumbering rush. They had to get this over quickly because it wouldn't be long before someone raised an alarm. I side-stepped as he swung, but not as neatly as usual, and again came the sickening pain in my shoulder. As I jerked round in an attempt to ride the blow, I brought my toe up against his knee-cap as hard as I could. He yelped, but I hadn't time to feel pleased because the other guy was crowding up on me again. I ducked very low and brought my right fist into his groin as he went past.

Suddenly Roxanne was there.

'Beat it,' I shouted, but only a croak came out. I was down on one knee.

For an answer she stepped between me and the first thug who was edging up more cautiously. He paused, uncertain of this new complication, but his buddy had no such niceties. In he came at Roxanne with his head down. He might have been thinking she'd get

47

out of the way. Instead, she waited until he was three feet away, then brought her pointed toe up into his face. He screamed with pain and stopped dead, hands to his face. Then Roxanne, whom I'd been so anxious to protect, chopped him either side of the head with the sides of her hands and he went down like a sack of coal. I was up now and moving after the other one. He stood his ground, measuring me. There were shouts from the street and a couple of people were heading towards us. The man looked across at the oncoming shadows, then suddenly made up his mind. He turned and made off between the parked cars. It suited me. I had to get out of there before any police turned up.

'Scott.'

It was Roxanne's voice. She had the motor running. I stumbled back to the car and climbed in beside her.

'Take off,' I muttered. 'Don't use any lights.'

We moved away. A couple of startled faces loomed towards us out of the darkness and quickly receded as we shot by. Once we hit the main thoroughfare, I leaned across and flipped on the lights. Roxanne was handling the car like an expert. I chuckled.

'What's the joke?' she asked.

'I was just thinking.'

What I'd been thinking was that the first thing flashing through my mind when the car-park skiffle group went for me, was that

Roxanne had set me up for it. It's so old, it's tired, but I really thought it just the same. Twenty seconds later she'd saved me from a very bad beating, and it all goes to show you shouldn't jump to conclusions. What puzzled me was, who were those guys, and why pick on me?

'Are you feeling better?' Her voice was concerned.

'Fine, thanks.'

It was the shortest answer I could think of. How I really felt was terrible. The passenger seat in that car had always seemed like the last word in luxury, but I could find no position which was half-way comfortable. Everything ached down my back and left side. I was also feeling confused about several things, such as the reason for the attack, Roxanne's proficiency in dealing with it, and her willingness to get away from the spot without hollering for the law. Probably more than anything else I was annoyed with myself for being caught that way. Twelve months ago those two characters wouldn't have got within a mile of me. I thought about Rourke, and his doubts about me, and that didn't cheer me up one little bit.

Roxanne sat beside me, saying nothing. She was concentrating on her driving, and several times I looked at her serene face, wondering just what she was thinking. I was wondering a couple of other things, too, which were more

49

concerned with that part of the evening which was yet to come.

'Which way from here?' she suddenly asked.

I told her, and five minutes later we stepped out into the garage on the corner of Quiet Square. Roxanne walked slowly beside me down the street, deep in thoughts of her own. I had an eye skinned for the man in the raincoat. He wasn't on view, but at the far corner a small, black sedan was parked and I caught the glow of a cigarette from the back seat. Almost certainly my admirer from earlier on. When we reached my place, there was no shilly-shally about whether or not Roxanne was coming in. She was coming in, she knew it and I knew it. I closed the door, flicked switches down and said:

'Let me take your wrap.'

It wasn't really a wrap, just one of those lengths of filmy material women throw around their shoulders towards the end of a hot evening.

'This is quite nice.' She waved an arm around.

'Glad you like it.'

I got her sitting down and mixed a couple of drinks. Mine didn't need any mixing really, passing straight from the bottle to the glass to the throat. It was good. She sipped at her glass, nodded appreciation and said:

'You ought to have a look at that shoulder. Let me know if I can do anything to help.'

She was right. In the bathroom I took off my jacket and shirt. The movement of my arms hurt some, and as the shirt came off, I could see why. I seemed to be one big bruise on the left side, black, blue and red weals and lumps. I must have been very close to a busted shoulder back in that car park. As it was, I could count myself lucky, a few bruises never killed anybody. There was some liniment and stuff in the shaving cabinet. I fooled around with it as best I could, and it helped a little with some of the worst aches. When I went back to Roxanne, she was comfortably sitting back smoking quietly.

'Will you live?' she smiled.

'I'll issue a bulletin every four hours,' I replied. 'Roxanne, tell me something. Why were you in such a hurry to get away after that little mix-up tonight?'

She stubbed out the cigarette.

'Really, that's rather cool of you. It was quite obvious to anybody that I couldn't afford to be questioned over what I was doing in some sordid brawl outside a place like the Crinoline. You may not know who I am, but it should be clear even to you that my normal background isn't a pick-up bar of that type.' Her voice was edged with ice now, and of course as she spoke I realised it would have had to be something like that. She had some more to say. 'I hope you don't think your question is going to make me forget how anxious *you* were to get away from there? And please don't insult me by suggesting you were thinking of my good name.'

I shook my head.

'No. I didn't think about you at all. Look,' I fished around for my card, 'I'm a business man. My organisation is a very personal thing, as it suggests. Any breath of a thing of this kind could do me a lot of harm.'

She inspected the card with some care, looking from it to me with a look of serious consideration.

'But who were those men? Business rivals?'

I didn't know who they were. For a minute or two I put a lot of good effort into getting that point across. She began to believe me.

'And you. You were terrific. Where'd you learn that stuff?' I demonstrated the dropping routine to show what I meant.

'Oh, it was a couple of years ago now. Abroad.' She lifted out a silver cigarette case and passed it over. 'As an American, you may not have been particularly interested, but the great pastime in this country since the war has been to kow-tow to every miserable little State that decided to pull a gun on us. I happened to be in one of those places two years ago, and the British women were few in number. We all had to learn a good deal about self-defence in a hell of a hurry, and put it into effect soon afterwards. I remembered what I was taught.'

I'd have liked to ask for the rest of that

story, but it was clear that lid had been lifted only long enough to allow exactly that much information to escape, and now the hatches were battened down again. I noticed her glass was empty, and motioned towards it.

'Thank you. Could you make it a weak one, please, while I go and tidy my hair somewhere? I feel a mess.'

I showed her the bedroom, and made it a weak one, a very weak one. For Roxanne, that is. I felt I could still manage a proper drink. Glass in hand, I wandered to the window overlooking the square. I was just in time to see my friend in the raincoat walking towards the little black sedan. It was eight to five he'd taken a stroll as far as the garage to see whether my heap was tucked in for the night. Thinking about him and the two guys in the car park, I didn't hear Roxanne come back into the room.

'Losing interest?' came her voice.

I turned around to deny that, but the words stuck in my throat. She was wearing my dressing-gown gathered shapelessly round her. The deep black hair was brushed loosely out from her head. Her eyes were shining. Very carefully I set the glass down on the window ledge. As I pulled her towards me, she closed her eyes and swayed into my arms, moist lips parted. Softly she whispered:

'I always swore that if I ever did anything like this, some man would be very, very glad.'

Then she was hard against me, pressing and writhing. I slipped my hand between the folds of the dressing-gown. Inside there was only Roxanne.

CHAPTER THREE

'Are you ill, Mr. Stevens?'

My head felt uncomfortable. I reached around to punk up the pillow. There was no pillow. That annoyed me just enough to make me open one eye. A searing beam of sunlight burned into it. I closed it again quickly and lay still while the rest of me came to life. A voice, something about a voice.

'Mr. Stevens, please answer me.'

There it was again. I knew that voice, couldn't quite place it. Turning my head away from the direction I imagined the sun was coming I tried opening the eye again. There were white leather spike-heeled shoes, and slim tanned legs. Roxanne. I made a feeble attempt to grab for her.

'Pull yourself together Mr. Stevens.'

I had it now, Pat Richmond. Pat Richmond? What was my secretary doing here? She wasn't that kind of secretary. It was fairly clear that I was on the floor for some reason.

'Give me—give me a hand up will you Pat?'

With a sigh of relief she put an arm behind

my head and levered me up. Finally I made a sitting position. I had no jacket on but was otherwise fully dressed. My shoulder and side were hurting, but in that direction my head was way out in front. I didn't understand any of it. Pat was sitting on a low chair near me, watching anxiously.

'What're you doing here?' I asked ungraciously. She shrugged.

'Well, you left early yesterday because you weren't very well. Then this morning you didn't come to the office. I 'phoned several times and got no answer. Finally I thought you might be ill here by yourself. I took your spare key from the drawer and—and, well here I am.'

'This morning?' 'Phone?' I looked at my strap watch. The hands pointed to twelve-thirty. That couldn't be right, it must have stopped. When I held it to my ear all it said was tick-tick-tick.

'Can you make coffee, Pat?' She nodded. 'Then please do. Very strong.' She stepped daintily away. Give you an idea how bad I felt, I didn't even watch her walk. Any movement made my head feel like somebody was kicking it. By the time I'd got to a chair I could sympathise with a football after a big game. After an unsuccessful grope around for a cigarette I had a think back. A little over twelve hours before I had started some high-powered dalliance with a lady who told me her name was Roxanne Baxter. Only, as it began to get interesting I began to pass out. Yeah, that was it. It was clearer now. I had passed out on Roxanne. Passing out is something I don't make a habit of, and the reason I'd done it last night was because the highly desirable Roxanne had put a little extra something in my drink to give it a kick. Or more accurately to give me a kick—in the back of the head. Why? Had I picked up a kind of lady burglar? No, I decided. Whatever her game was, that wasn't it. I was making a lot of no progress when Pat Richmond arrived with the coffee and two small white tablets. I looked at the tablets, then Pat. Suspiciously both times.

'What are these?'

'They'll make you feel better Mr. Stevens. If anything can.'

My secretary isn't the kind of girl who sniffs, but there was a sniff somewhere around those last three words.

'Listen, if you think I was drunk you're wrong. I picked up a couple of crab sandwiches while I was out last night. They didn't hit it off with what I was drinking, that's all.'

'I see. So in fact you're suffering from a kind of food poisoning?'

'Er, yeah, that's it. Kind of a food poisoning.'

The coffee was good. When I was halfway through she reminded me about the tablets. I swallowed them down.

'Thank you Nurse Richmond.'

Nurse smiled. Pat is one of those cool English beauties you hear so much about. When I say cool I don't refer to her temperament, just the appearance side. As to the rest I don't know. Not that I haven't thought sometimes it might be nice finding out, but I just don't happen to think it's a good idea to get involved personally with people from the organisation. So as I say she's cool. Crisp too, but not even, except in temperament. She has ash blonde hair brushed away from the forehead, grey eyes and one of those pale complexions that some people might consider fragile. At the moment she was wearing a bright red blouse, white linen skirt caught at the waist with a two-inch black belt. Those uneven parts we were just talking about were right where they ought to be, only more so. And no jewellery. Pat Richmond, I hate to say it again, looked cool.

I emptied the cup.

'More coffee?' she asked.

I shook my head.

'No thanks honey. What I really need right now is a bath and some fresh clothes. You get back to the office and front for me, huh? I'll be in this afternoon.'

'Very well.'

'And thanks for picking me up off the floor.'

She didn't hang around with a lot of

woman's talk about would I be all right? etc. If I wanted anything I'd ask for it, and she would do it. That's one big advantage a paid secretary has over a dame whose interest is romantic. She doesn't fuss.

While I lay in the tub I was interested in two things. First the Rover boys of the night before. Who sent them after me and why? If I knew who, I could probably work out the why all by myself. Secondly there was Roxanne, and the people who sent her. I knew why. In roaming around the place I'd noticed things which were no longer quite in their proper places. The lady had searched the joint, turned it upside down. I doubted whether she'd been looking for any particular object. Nobody had entrusted me with a gem-encrusted idol stolen from mad priests in India, not even a map of Treasure Island. It seemed to me that she had been trying to find out what sort of guy I was, what interested me, what private papers I might keep around. That's just how it seemed to me, and I wouldn't have thought of that, but for Rourke. If there was anything to his theory that somebody had plans for Senator Edward P. Masters they would be taking an interest in the movements of Raymond Bentley. The people Bentley got in touch with would also come in for examination, and that would include me. They hadn't done me any harm after all. Just let me get nice and close to a beautiful woman, then put me to sleep for a few hours. On balance I had no complaints. In fact I rather liked the method. Even if I was as innocent as I wanted them to think, I'd be unlikely to complain to the law. I couldn't hold back a wry grin at the thought of the look I'd get from the station sergeant if I went to him with my tale.

'You see Sergeant, I picked up this girl—'

'Where sir?' Polite enquiry.

'Er—the Crinoline.'

'I see.'

'We had some drinks, and went back, to my place. Er—that is—'

'I quite understand sir.'

'Then I passed out—that is my drink was drugged—'

'Yes, sir.'

'And this morning, when I woke up, she was gone.'

Pause.

'Anything missing sir? Any valuables, jewellery, cash?'

'Well—um—no.'

'I see sir. Now this drugging. Very serious. You have the glass containing some of the drugged liquid?'

And, of course, I hadn't. Roxanne had carefully rinsed and dried both glasses, and although I wasn't going to bother to check, I was quite sure that not one whorl of any of her fingerprints was on view anywhere in the apartment. I was nicely compromised, if innocent. If everyone Bentley had contacted last night had been handled as expertly as Simple Scott Stevens, it was evident that the organisation was large, and competent. But that didn't answer the outstanding question. If the people after Masters had sent Roxanne, who had organised the attack in the car-park? It was possible for the attack to have been fake in order to put Roxanne in solid with me. Possible, but far too complicated. She was in solid enough the moment I laid eyes on her, and the people who sent her would have been confident of that, or got another girl. I gave that one up for a while.

On the way to the office I picked up an afternoon paper. The front was mainly taken up with the arrival of one Senator Masters at London Airport. There was a lot of chatter about his background, old stuff dug out of the files and served with a new sauce. It was eight to five the whole story had been written last week and a space left for the photograph. The greater part of the picture was taken up by the aircraft he'd arrived in, and the lines of officials waiting to receive him. I wanted to get a close look at the man in whose service I'd already collected a few bruises and a headache, but the photograph wasn't clear enough for that. I could see a tall, square, confident man, waving gaily for the cameras as he stepped down from the aircraft. Details were blurred, and the inset close-up of his face wasn't a great improvement. I thought I'd defer judgment until we met that night.

On the inside pages I did come across a little item about an attack on a man in a car-park outside a well-known club. The man, evidently a foreigner, had been set upon by four other men, who drove away in a car when people ran to help. The police were anxious to interview a tall man with a black moustache, who seemed to be the leader of the attackers. The victim had apparently, also left without giving his name. I was a cop myself once, and let me say now, it's no, fun trying to catch up with criminals on the bum descriptions you get from reliable witnesses.

Pat Richmond was behind her desk, head bent over some paper work when I wandered in.

'Hallo,' she greeted. 'How's the—um—food poisoning?'

'A little better thanks. Must have been those tablets of yours.'

'Good. There's been a man on the telephone twice wanting to talk to you. A Mr. Stavros.'

'Mr. Who?'

'Stavros. S-T-A-V-R-O-S. Would like you to call him back. I have the number here.' She indicated a note pad.

Thoughtfully I picked up the pad. Mr. Stavros operated from a Euston telephone, whatever that might mean. Pat Richmond

61

watched me without great curiosity.

'Who is this guy? Do we know him?'

She shook her head.

'Not in my time. He may have done business with us in the old days.'

I grinned at her. La Richmond had been with me seven months. Her opinions of the way certain records had been maintained prior to her arrival was no secret. In fact all activities of the organisation which took place before she came had occurred in the 'old days'. A stranger might have a dim picture of rusty clerks in high wing collars, but just for the record the 'old days' had ended seven months before.

'I'll call him later. Coupla things I want to do first.'

In my office I began to check on Mr. Stavros. The Post Office telephone directory entry read:

STAVROS, D. Sec. Freedom Council, Freedom House, Euston Road.

That told me which volume to reach for next. You'd be surprised at the annual bill I get for directories of one kind and another, but it's the only way to keep information up to date. I thumbed through the pages. This one said:—

FREEDOM COUNCIL, The
    Add. Freedom House, Euston Road, N.
    Sec. D. Stavros Founded 1949. Objects:
    To promote the interests of refugees

from terrorism, and in particular those from Communist countries. Also to aid oppressed peoples in any part of the world. Contributions and Enquiries: Secretary c/o above address.

From another book I found that Stavros had a first name, and that Dimitri Stavros was thirty-eight years old and a naturalised Englishman. That was all I could find about the man, but there was plenty of stuff about his outfit, the Freedom Council. They were a militant, not to say military, anti-Red crowd, always on the lookout for a chance to upset the Commies some way or other. They even had a reception-centre down in Sussex. I began to think I was looking forward to my telephone call. I dialled the Euston number. After a while there was some clicking, and a guttural voice said:

'Freedom House.'

I told him I wanted Mr. Stavros, and he said who was I, and I told him that, then there was more clicking, then another voice said:

'Stavros. Am I speaking to Mr. Scott Stevens?'

Nothing guttural about this character. This was one of those accents straight from a Continental movie actor, the kind the girls go for.

'Yeah, I'm Stevens, what can I do for you?'

He wanted me to go see him, and after a

little hedging and stalling around I said O.K. and we made it for four-thirty. With the 'phone back in the cradle I spent ten minutes thinking about what friend Stavros wanted with me. Then I went and told Pat Richmond it had been a mistake to come to the office, especially in that heat, and went down to the street to find a taxi. The driver dropped me outside Freedom House at four twenty-eight. I didn't find out much from staring at the front of the building, except that it was built of that dirty grey stone so familiar in London. The list of organisations housed inside was formidable, and every one had something like International, or Friendly or Anti- in its title. The Freedom Council rated the whole of the ground floor and that made them the top anti-lists on view. A dark sallow girl with a bun and no make-up sat behind a sign which invited enquiries. I enquired for Stavros, and a minute later a young guy of around twenty-five came out.

'I am Kulbin, Mr. Stavros' personal assistant.'

He was fair, crew-cut, dark business suit, spectacles with a thick tortoiseshell frame. Mr. Kublin was evidently very earnest. I followed him down a passage, past several doors, and finally into a small room where a girl sat behind a typewriter. This one had brown hair but could otherwise have been the sister of the one in the hall. She watched without apparent interest as Kulbin opened a door just beyond her desk, and motioned me in.

'Mr. Stevens,' he announced, then closed the door behind me. The furniture was plain, the decor was plain, the fittings unexciting. But I didn't get around to any of that for a while. My attention was focused on the man who rose from behind the desk. Not much over medium height, Stavros was handsome in a heavy-featured way. His double-breasted suit had cost money, so had the shirt and tie. He seemed to exude a restless vitality, you could feel the strength and purpose driving this man. Whatever else he might be, Dimitri Stavros was not the one to sit in a dingy office waiting for a few charitable contributions to arrive from conscience-stricken industrialists. His hand was hard and a little rough to my surprise, a hand which had been other places than a manicure parlour.

'Mr. Stevens, it is good of you to come. Please sit down.'

I mumbled something and sat facing him.

'If you would wish to smoke, please do. Myself, I do not have the habit.'

I decided I would wish to smoke. He edged an ash-tray towards me, then clasped his hands on the desk before him and studied me carefully before speaking. I smoked and waited.

'Mr. Stevens, I asked you to come here for a special reason. A very special reason.'

I nodded.

'The world today, it is in two camps. There can be no alternative points of view. There are Communists. There are anti-Communists. The Freedom Council, of which I am honoured to be secretary, is prominent, not to say the most important, among anti-Communist organisations.'

He paused. There didn't seem to be a lot I could add to that. I tapped some cigarette-ash into the tray.

'I believe you are not a Communist, Mr. Stevens?'

I was determined not to let this guy annoy me. I replied:

'I'm an American, Mr. Stavros. We don't go in for that kind of stuff.'

'Precisely. However, it would be going too far, if I say that you are anti-Communist.'

'Now look—' I began.

'No, you look Mr. Stevens.' He shouted me down. 'You are non-Communist, not the same thing at all. The Americans, the English,' he waved his arms, 'I despair of them. Asleep in a violent world, blind to what happens under their noses. Non-Communist, certainly, and yet permitting these swine to organise openly in their midst. Entertaining their executioners at state banquets. Shaking hands with the men who one day, and one day not too far off, will give the order for their extermination.'

'We might have a little something to say

about that, when and if the time comes.'

Dammit, I had to get a word in somewhere.

'The time is now. Here. Today.'

He made one of those dramatic pauses, but I wasn't going to wait for him this time.

'Look, what is all this leading to?'

'Of course. Forgive me. Sometimes my emotions get the better of me.'

That I doubted. For my dough this Stavros was a smart character, and not likely to let his emotions or anything else take charge of his tongue. I'd been supposed to hear just what I had heard. Stavros smoothed the hair at the side of his head. He was ready to get down to cases now.

'Today a true friend of the people arrived in England. I refer to Senator Masters, that great American. You are aware of this. You are also aware of other matters, because I advised Mr. Bentley to speak with you.'

'You?'

He nodded.

'But I understood from Bentley it was Masters' own idea to hire me while he was over here.'

'Quite so. It is as you say. However,' he shrugged, 'Mr. Bentley would naturally come to me about such an important matter. I confirmed with him that in my opinion you should prove satisfactory.'

'Thanks,' I said, without much conviction. 'Now would you mind telling me just why you should be consulted about such a thing?'

'Very well.' I hadn't ruffled Stavros one hair's breadth. 'It was at the suggestion of my Council that Senator Masters decided to come to Europe. Naturally there has been considerable negotiation in diplomatic circles, but the Senator is a very determined man. At his personal insistence my Council has been kept informed of developments, and even taken into conference concerning his itinerary.'

It figured too. Everybody I'd talked with so far agreed that Masters was a bullhead, and if he had decided that this Freedom Council could be a force in his anti-Red drive, he would have his own way about consulting them. Stavros was still talking.

'So it was natural for Mr. Bentley to advise me of the Senator's intentions with regard to his—ah—free time.'

'I see. Would you mind also telling me what makes you think I'm capable of doing what's wanted?'

'I have heard of you Mr. Stevens. Once or twice your name has been mentioned by various people. Always I am left with an impression of a man of resource, a man not a stranger to violence. Of course I had no personal knowledge of you. I arranged for that to be rectified last night.'

'Last night?' Suddenly I began to see. Angrily I said: 'If you mean those two thugs were sent after me by you, I'll—'

He raised his hands, palms towards me.

'Please. It was necessary. I beg you accept my deepest apologies. Of course, the men went much too far. Under such circumstances, you appreciate, one's temper—'

'Appreciate? Yeah, I appreciate. I was there, friend. What the hell's the idea?'

'I assure you, Mr. Stevens, I am deeply pained to make this confession to you. But it was necessary.'

'Necessary?'

'Of course. Tonight, tomorrow, you may be required to defend the life of Senator Masters, a man whose importance in the fight against the Communists cannot be measured. Would you expect me to risk such a responsibility in the hands of a man I have no knowledge of?'

'But those guys were going to kill me,' I spluttered.

'No. They would have beaten you and left.' He could see I wasn't at all mollified by his sweet reasoning tone. 'Mr. Stevens, I have apologised. I do so again. But please, put yourself in my position.'

I was trying, and he could see that.

'A few bruises Mr. Stevens are not to be weighed on the same scale as the life of Senator Masters. Nor, if it became necessary, is your life. You see, I am quite frank with you.'

I had to hand it to the guy. He certainly laid

it on the line when he did start talking.

'It's a comfort to know how important I am in your eyes,' I said bitterly.

'We must speak frankly as men. I have my job to do, you yours. You will be paid, well paid.'

I shook my head.

'Not enough. There isn't so much money that I'll get myself killed for it. I'm just an ordinary joe, Mr. Stavros. I contracted with Bentley to keep an eye on the Senator. If there's a little rough stuff, well O.K. I've had some before. But I'm not going to sit still while people try to kill me. I didn't make that kind of deal, and I'm not making one now.'

It sounded reasonable. I wasn't telling Stavros or anybody else my business. To him I was kind of a guide and bodyguard on salary, and guys like that don't get themselves killed if they can avoid it. Stavros stared at me coolly for a few moments, then:

'I see. I do not find it possible to admire you Mr. Stevens, but at least you are open with me. It is vital in these matters to know the unreliable people in a crisis. It is as I said earlier, I think. You are non-Communist, an important difference from an Anti-Communist.'

The tone was edged. Not for the first time in circumstances like that, I wanted to get up, stick my chest out, strut around shouting what a good American I was. Just let them li'l ole

70

Commies get near ole Scott Stevens and you'd see something. Yessir, them yellerbellies better not come too close—and so on. I don't usually talk that way, nor even think like it, but it's a slimy kind of feeling just to sit there while some guy tells you about the rubber content in your spinal region. Still, that's just one of the joys of life when you're one of the family. It was simply that I hadn't had to take that kind of stuff lately.

'I don't mean to be offensive Mr. Stevens. You do not think as we think, and after all, that is democracy, is it not? I am sure we shall find you most satisfactory up to the line you have drawn. You will be interested to know that one of the men who attacked you will be unable to appear in public for several weeks.'

'If you're waiting for me to say I'm sorry, you're out of luck. How about the other guy?'

He fluttered his hands.

'A few bruises, a headache. Nothing more. He mentioned a lady—?'

'Yeah, there was a lady with me. It was her put your boy under wraps, not me.'

'So I believe. The man was stupid. He exceeded his instructions. After you demonstrated your capabilities, the men were to have left. As to attacking a lady, I give you my word I was shocked.' He really meant it.

'Don't worry about it. She didn't get a scratch.'

'Excellent. A most resourceful young

woman, I am told. Is she perhaps, a special friend?'

'Yup, a special friend.'

He could see I wasn't going to elaborate on that, so he changed the subject.

'I am glad we have talked Mr. Stevens. I feel the air is now clear. Please do not feel too alone in this matter. Mr. Bentley will be keeping me advised of the Senator's movements. There will be additional assistance to hand should it be required.'

'Good.'

I got up from the chair.

'I am afraid we may not have met under the best of circumstances Mr. Stevens. Perhaps if you had some idea of the work of this great movement you would understand more easily. The Senator is to attend a rally which the Council has arranged for tomorrow. I would like you to come and see for yourself. You will feel the great strength of our people, see how they admire a fighter like the Senator. You may even see why you have those bruises.'

He smiled slightly at the last part, and I grinned back ruefully.

'That is something I'd like to understand Mr. Stavros. Where is this meeting?'

'At the Albert Hall. At two-thirty in the afternoon.'

'How'll I get in? I don't belong to anything.'

He held out a white card. It was headed 'Freedom Council' gave the date and time of the rally. There was a number printed up in the top right hand corner—619.

'That will get you in, never fear. And the number will tell the staff there where you are to sit.'

I stuck the card in my billfold.

'Wouldn't it be easier to have row letters and numbers the way they do for a concert?' I queried.

'Easier? No,' he told me. 'With lettering people can work out for themselves where they are to sit. If they feel they are not close enough to the front they start to protest. Everybody wants to feel his contribution is so much more than everybody elses. Everybody thinks he should be in the front row. My staff here is small. They cannot spend all day arguing with ticket holders about where they are to sit. This way nobody knows until he gets there. Then it is too late for talk.'

He had a point there.

'O.K. Mr. Stavros, I'll be there. Should be interesting.'

'Interesting,' he repeated. 'Interesting. Perhaps that is all it will be to you. To everyone else it will be a time of triumph, a great feeling of strength and purpose. But to you it will be only interesting. Ah well, perhaps that is at least a step forward.'

I got out of there before he tried signing me up for something. The young guy Kulbin was hanging around outside waiting to show me out.

'He talks up a storm, your boss,' I told him.

Kulbin didn't get that at all. He screwed up his face in puzzlement. In his clipped careful English he said:

'I am sorry, but I do not comprehend.'

'Mr. Stavros,' I explained, 'He gets kind of worked up about this organisation. You know, enthusiastic.'

I was getting to him now. The face cleared, and he nodded seriously.

'Dimitri Stavros is a wonderful man. A fighter. He is like a beacon to this great movement. You are thinking of joining us?'

'Well—er—no. Not exactly. I'm just kind of taking an interest, you know, getting to know how the movement works. How about you, you just work here, or are you a voluntary helper?'

'Ah yes. You mean, is this my employment? Yes, it is. My salary you understand, is very small. It pains me that I must accept any payment but—' he shrugged, 'One must have food in the stomach, a bed. For this one must pay.'

'Naturally.'

We were at the street door now.

'I'm coming to the rally tomorrow,' I told him. 'Maybe I'll see you there.'

'Perhaps,' he smiled.

There didn't seem to be a cruising cab on view. I walked along thinking about Stavros and his Freedom Council. Two things I knew for sure. Stavros was a very determined character. You don't casually send out two guys to beat up another simply in order to find out how tough he is. It takes a special kind of toughness, and that Stavros had. One other thing I knew, or could now guess. If Stavros, with all his knowledge about how the game was played, thought it was necessary to set the dogs on me, just to test me out, it meant the other team would play very rough indeed. I didn't feel any better about the bruises, but at least I was getting the general idea. These guys were playing for real, and maybe the little one-round preliminary the night before would tone me up, help to get me in shape for the main event. If I was good enough to enter, that was. Privately I had to admit I hadn't made much of a showing so far.

CHAPTER FOUR

At eleven that night I nosed out of the home-going traffic and pulled up outside the brand new sixteen-storey Skyroof Hotel. London has been getting up to date lately hotel-wise, and the Skyroof was the most recent to open its door to the famous and wealthy people who could afford the fare. A dignified man in a royal blue uniform with white gloves opened the door for me to get out. He made me feel shabby. 'Shall you be staying long enough for me to park the car, sir?

'Be here about twenty minutes,' I told him.

As I walked across the floodlit forecourt he snapped his gloved hand and a young guy in blue overalls appeared from somewhere, hopped into the car and drove it round the corner.

Inside I went up to the desk and said I'd come to visit Senator Masters. The elegant man behind the counter studied me carefully.

'What name shall I say, sir?'

I told him and he consulted something which rested on a shelf below the counter on his side.

'Ah yes sir. The Senator is expecting you.'

Looking over my shoulder he nodded, and I turned to find two men coming towards me. There was a twenty year gap in their ages, otherwise you couldn't put a pin between them. They were tall men with powerful bodies and hard eyes. They wore quiet business suits, and they moved lightly as ballet dancers.

'Good evening sir,' said the older man. 'I believe you are calling on Senator Masters?'

'Why yes,' I tried to look mildly surprised, 'Is it against the law?'

The young one smiled but his eyes were still like grey flints.

'Why do you say that sir? About the law, I mean?'

'Because you're some kind of cops,' I explained gently. 'That much I can see.'

'Very observant, sir,' said the first one. 'Would you mind if we had a few words with you before you call on the Senator?'

Would I mind, he said.

'How do you mean, would I mind? Is there a choice?' I demanded.

He smiled tightly and stood to one side so I could walk between them. They led me to a small private office behind the reception desk.

'All right, what happens now?' I asked.

The younger one replied.

'Nothing unusual Mr. Stevens. We have a note that you are expected here this evening—'

'Then why all this Gestapo bit?' I cut in.

'Because,' he explained patiently, 'All we know is that Mr. Stevens is coming. We don't know you. There's someone coming down. He knows Stevens, and if you're the right man, that's all there is to it.'

'O.K.' I nodded. Then a thought struck me. 'Say, supposing I'm not Stevens?'

The older one took care of that

'It will be much easier for everyone if you are,' he replied.

I'll bet, I thought privately. They were polite, these two. I knew the breed from way back. Polite, and tough when it got necessary.

'You're an American, Mr. Stevens,' observed the young one. 'Sorry that we have to do this, but don't forget the Senator is a very prominent fellow-countryman of yours. You would hate to feel that we didn't take proper care of him over here, I'm sure.'

He had me there. I just nodded, and we all stood there waiting. Another minute or two went by then the door opened and Bentley came in. He looked at me quickly then nodded to the others.

'He's Stevens,' he announced. Then to me, 'Glad you're on time.'

'I would have been early,' I replied, 'But we were having such a lovely chat.'

The others grinned and went away. Bentley took me out of the office and towards some elevators at the rear of the building.

'The Senator is looking forward to seeing you,' he remarked conversationally. 'If I'd filled his programme today I'd be asleep in bed by this time. But not Edward P. He's even talking about a gin-rummy session after you've gone.'

There was no attendant at the elevator. We got in and Bentley pushed a button. We moved up fast, so fast my stomach forgot momentarily we were supposed to go upwards. In a very few seconds we were at the twelfth floor.

'This way.'

I followed him past two men who sat sweating in thick blue suits opposite the elevator shaft. They ignored Bentley but their eyes raked over me like X-rays. Bentley stopped at a door on which hung silver numbers, a four and a one. Here he knocked and a man looked out immediately. I didn't know it was a man right away. All I saw was a glittering eye and a section of nose. Then there was a grunt from behind the nose and the door was closed again. There was a scraping as a chained bolt slid along its housing, then the door opened wider and we could go in. Again I was subjected to a searching stare, from the man behind the door. He looked like the others, powerful, watchful, suspicious.

'This is Mr. Stevens, Thomson,' Bentley told him.

Thomson nodded at me but didn't speak. I nodded back. He seemed to be the last of the private army. Next stop was the great man himself. We went into the next room. He was sitting in a deep chair, surrounded by opened newspapers. As we entered he looked up, screwed up the paper he'd been reading and threw it after the others. Then he got up and I took my first look at the man who was causing all the hooha.

Senator Masters was even bigger than his pictures, about six two and packing more than two twenty pounds at a guess. He had short black hair which wasn't going to be told what to do by any brush, and eyebrows that bristled. The rugged face was tanned a rich red and his eyes sparked from fleshy folds.

'You're Stevens, huh?'

He stuck out a large hand and barked at me. I took the hand and was careful to adjust my fingers for what I felt sure was coming. He gripped hard, then harder. I was glad I'd thought about the fingers, as I squeezed back. The veins on his thick neck stood out as he put on pressure. I knew I wouldn't be able to win this contest, so I tried to bluff my way out. I grinned at him. He chuckled and let go.

'Not bad Stevens, not bad,' he mumbled. 'Back where I come from that's a great game on a Saturday night.'

'I couldn't have taken much more, Senator,' I admitted. He shook his head.

'Nix on that Senator,' he roared. 'Everybody calls me Ed. Well siddown, siddown. You're Scott, that right?'

'That's right Sen—Ed,' I corrected.

I parked opposite and had a better look at him. Bradley was right about the suspenders. These were an offensive blue, with harem girls picked out in yellow. He caught my glance and stuck a thumb under one side, slapping the elastic band against his chest.

'Pretty nice huh? How'd you like to be me, eh? Have half a dozen of these little beauties climbing all over you at the same time?'

I managed a grin. This man was a senator, I reminded myself. Never mind if he looked and acted like a travelling salesman. Never mind if his gags and the rest of him were thirty years out of date. This was all surface stuff.

Underneath there had to be more, plenty more. You don't get to where Masters had just by acting like a fill-in comic in some mid-west burlesque house. That's what I kept telling myself.

'Well, what d'ya say Ray, does old Scott here get a drink?'

Bentley nodded.

'Certainly, Senator. What'll it be Stevens?'

I told him to make it scotch and plain water. Masters grinned and slapped himself on the leg.

'Scotch for old Scott, eh? Hey maybe that's how you came by the name, huh? Maybe that was all you'd take as a baby. Wouldn't go for that milk even then, huh?'

He was having a whale of a time evidently. Bentley brought over my drink, and Masters frowned at him.

'Scott will you tell this guy to be more friendly to me? All this time we been working together, and still he gives me that Senator routine.'

Bentley smiled.

'I'm sorry Ed. It slips out sometimes.'

'Makes a man feel like he's with strangers, Ray,' grumbled the big man. 'How'sa drink Scott?'

'Fine, thank you er, Ed,' I told him.

'Good, good. Well now, let's get down to business. What can you do to liven up a tired old politician in this town?' Without waiting for a reply he stuck out a hand, pointing at me. 'And let me warn you in advance, I have seen some entertainment in my time. Take a lot of living up to, so this better be good.'

I'd already formed an impression of exactly what the Senator had in mind, but that was based on second-hand information. Now was the time to find out for certain. I started off carefully, naming one or two of the better night spots and took it from there. He asked questions about each place, dismissed it on some grounds or other. Soon I found we were talking about places a little further down the scale, then further than that. Bentley didn't interrupt once, and it was hard to judge from that impassive face, just what was going on in his mind. Probably nothing, I reasoned, He'd heard the same conversation a dozen times, in a dozen hotel rooms. He knew what the Senator was after, knew that all the by-play meant nothing. He might not have a very high opinion of Masters' tastes, but he was familiar with them by now.

Finally I was dredging up places even the police hadn't found out about yet. The Senator's interest heightened noticeably, and I was repelled by the eager anticipation on his face as he pressed me for details of what he called the 'fun' available. In the end he settled for Irish Mollie's, a place not normally famous as a rendezvous for visiting politicians. We would leave the hotel at about eleven the

82

following night, and in the meantime I wasn't to breathe a word to anyone about our destination. He needn't have said that. If I hadn't got to make my official report, I wouldn't have let anybody know I proposed to visit Irish Mollie's. Some of my acquaintances are not too particular, but everybody has a limit. Irish Mollie's was over the limit for most people.

After we'd fixed up for the next night, Masters was plainly anxious to be rid of me. He lost all the forced good humour very quickly, and finally said:

'Well now look here, Scott boy, it's getting kind of late. Ray and me, we gotta sort through a whole stack of paper before we hit the sack. You won't mind if I kind of toss you out now huh, Scott?'

I got up at once.

'Why no, Ed. Sure. See you tomorrow night, then?'

'Huh? Oh, yeah tomorrow. And remember, don't breathe a word.'

I nodded. Bentley got up too.

'I'll come down with you. Without an escort this place is as hard to get out of as in.'

I said goodnight to Masters but he took no notice. As we walked along the corridor I said to Bentley:

'By the way, your boss has some rough friends.'

I told him about my talk with Dimitri

Stavros that afternoon, and the fight the previous night at the Crinoline. He listened carefully.

'Stavros is a very determined man,' he said finally. 'I think he went a little too far last night, but he only has the Senator's best interest at heart.'

If those monkeys had got to me the way they meant to, the only thing I'd have had at heart would have been a funeral procession, with Stavros as the star attraction,' I told him.

'I can understand how you feel. Tell me, this girl, Baxter. How do you suppose she got on to you so quickly?'

'I don't know. There's been a man watching my place since yesterday. I don't know what time he got started, but the first time I noticed him was a little while after you left.'

He made a face.

'So they could have simply followed me, left a man at each place I visited?'

'Could be.'

We were back at street level now. As we walked towards the bright-lit entrance, Bentley said:

'You seem to have got off to a rough start, Stevens. Sorry things have gone this way, but you begin to have an idea of what I was telling you about last night.'

'Better than an idea,' I informed him tersely. 'My ribs'll be blue for a week.'

He grinned.

'What a lucky thing you're in such fine physical shape.'

And that was all the sympathy I was going to get from that quarter. We said goodnight and I went outside. Nobody tried to jump me, nobody even so much as looked at me. Except that is the Gorgeous George in the blue uniform. He looked and kept right on looking until I'd deposited a large silver coin in the palm of the beautiful white gloved hand.

Well, that's democracy, I reflected as I started the car. When the door flunkey had finished for the night he'd no doubt go home in his Rolls Royce, and there'd probably be a chauffeur too, who'd open the door for *him*.

I headed home to Quiet Square to file my report before going to bed.

CHAPTER FIVE

As soon as I got home I dialled the Grosvenor number and went into my act. I thought it was a good report. Economical, concise and crisply presented. Well hell, somebody had to think well of it. The man at the other end didn't exactly turn handsprings. I collected my usual bag of grunts and clicks. Only this time I had a surprise. After I'd finished with all the facts I said:

'What about this Albert Hall rally? Do I

go?'

For once my anonymous admirer was at a loss. There was a pause, then he said:

'Hold it.'

I held it. I held it for what seemed like an hour, but was actually six or seven minutes. Then he came back on.

'Jeremy?'

'Still here,' I told him.

'You can go.'

And that was that. I put the receiver down, feeling slightly irritable. An irrational reaction, because what did I expect after all? The guy could scarcely be expected to swap the latest yarns with me. But just the same it was all very impersonal. Back in the old days, the telephone report gag was exactly the same, but at least I knew a lot of people then. Knew who was working with me, or at least what departments were involved. Now I was like a—like a waiter who had to deliver a perfect dinner to a private suite, then leave it outside the door without having the satisfaction of seeing the diner's appreciation. Or even what the girl looked like.

And speaking of girls, I wondered if I'd ever see Roxanne Baxter again. Probably not, I decided. Taking it as a whole, that was a very good thing. But on one count it was a very great shame. In my book, Roxanne owed me something, and I had a very precise idea of what it was.

Looking around at the empty apartment, I chuckled. It was past midnight, and I had better get any thoughts along those lines out of my head. For tonight at least. I wondered what would have been next in a Rick Bradford novel. Rick is my favourite character and probably yours too. He has a whale of a time, killing off the baddies, soaking himself in Napoleon brandy, and rolling in the hay with all the upper crust debs. Old Rick wouldn't be stuck for action like I was. Even if he did find himself alone in his apartment at midnight, there'd be a ring on the buzzer and he'd curse and open the door, and there she'd be. Five five, wet sensuous mouth, body writhing at him, the spoiled daughter of an oil tycoon. Yeah, I sighed, Rick knew how to live.

There was a ring at the buzzer. I gasped, took a quick look in the mirror, straightened my tie. Then I went to the door, curled my lip in a Rick-like nonchalance, and opened it.

Not five five at all. Five ten. Not twenty-two years old. More like fifty-two. And not even she, but he.

'Mr. Stevens?

He was smooth. Charcoal grey suit, striped silk tie. Grey hair, brushed back at the sides, small moustache to match.

'I'm Stevens,' I admitted.

'I wonder if I might come in and talk to you for a few moments Mr. Stevens?'

'It's after midnight,' I pointed out.

'Yes, I'm sorry about that. Actually I've been waiting outside since half-past ten. You only came home a few minutes ago.'

He hadn't got a gun, anyway. That was a start. The beautiful suit would have shown quickly any nasty bulges of that kind. I stood to one side.

'I guess so,' I grumbled. 'If it's that important.'

He thanked me and stepped inside.

'You may as well sit down.'

'Thank you.'

Instead of sitting, he walked to the fireplace and looked at the picture hanging over it.

'Really very nice indeed,' he commented. 'A Degas isn't it?'

'I wouldn't know,' I told him. It just came with the joint.' He smiled politely and sat, taking care not to disturb the elegant creasing of his pants.

'My name is Forrester,' he informed me, 'Charles Forrester. It is probably unfamiliar to you.'

Forrester. I fed it into the machine and waited. All that came out was blank tape.

'Sorry, you got me,' I confessed.

'I'm delighted to hear it, Mr. Stevens. It is no part of my duties to become well-known.'

'And what would your duties be exactly?' I questioned.

He reached inside his jacket and took out a slim gold cigarette case. I refused, saying I'd already smoked enough for one day. What I really meant was I wasn't going to take a chance on his cigarettes until I knew a lot more about him. And those 'duties'. I kept trying to think of who this man reminded me of, and suddenly I had it. Bentley. Forrester was a kind of English Bentley.

'I work for the British Government, Mr. Stevens. A kind of civil servant, if you like.'

I nodded, parked opposite him and waited for more. 'You've been to visit Senator Masters this evening,' he continued. 'Would you like to tell me why?'

'Would you like to tell me why I should?' I countered.

He nodded his head seriously.

'That's fair enough, I'd say. The Senator is a very big figure, politically. He is prominent largely for his—ah—critical attitude to certain powers. We feel a considerable responsibility, having such a figure over here. We feel it necessary to keep a very close watch on people who have dealings with him. The Senator is a very open-handed type of man, very hospitable by nature. It is not—ah—impossible that there could be people here who do not wish him well, Mr. Stevens. Our job is to try to ensure that any such people are not given an opportunity to—ah—give vent to their views too forcibly.'

I grinned.

'You're trying to tell me you think

somebody will try to bump him off. You're here to find out if it's me.'

He drew his lips into a prim line.

'Certainly it was not my intention to make either suggestion. The position simply is that we are charged with safeguarding the Senator's interest while he's a visitor to these shores.'

'There has to be more,' I pressed. 'Otherwise what are you doing here?'

He flicked ash into a tray by his hand.

'Mr. Stevens, I don't think we are going to achieve a proper understanding like this. Let me tell you a little more.'

'Do,' I encouraged.

Reaching in a pocket I dug out a pack of cigarettes and stuck one in my face. The movement was natural, almost automatic. I was putting a light to the thing before I recalled that I'd just refused Forrester.

'Mr. Stevens, I know who you are. I know about your business interests in this country, your Personal Service. I also know that you have been instrumental in providing, shall we say, certain extra services on one or two occasions when it looked as if one of your fellow-countrymen might get into trouble of some kind or another. Here or on the Continent.'

'I'm still listening.'

'I know more than that. You were a private detective in the United States before coming over here. Prior to that you served in the Army, and had a spell on Intelligence duty. I know a great many other things, too. Do you want to hear them all, or shall we take them as. read?'

I didn't want to hear them all. If Forrester said he knew them, he knew them. I've had enough experience of people to be able to tell that much. When he first arrived I'd been prepared to think I'd simply been tailed from the Skyroof Hotel, and was a new face. But this Forrester, and whoever he spoke for, had been on to me earlier.

Otherwise he couldn't have dug up all that stuff. The point was, how much earlier, and how did he latch on in the first place? Out loud, I said:

'I got the message. You know all about me. What happens now?'

'Now I'd like you to tell me what happened during your interview with the Senator.'

He ground out the half-smoked cigarette, carefully rubbed a shred of loose tobacco from his thumb, and waited. I sat and thought quickly about how much to tell this man. He was the voice of authority all right, that much I could tell. If I was what I claimed to be, an ordinary decent citizen carrying on a lucrative business, I wouldn't try to deceive him. I decided to give him the whole story, or what I hoped would sound like the whole story. I told him about Bentley's visit the night before, and

91

practically everything that had happened since. The thugs in the car park, Roxanne Baxter, Stavros and the Freedom Council. Everything up to and including my talk with Masters himself. Except that I didn't tell him we'd made an arrangement to go to Irish Mollie's. Forrester listened carefully to every word I said, never interrupting once. At the end he asked questions. Shrewd penetrating questions. Questions that back-tracked and criss-crossed. Questions that could only come from a highly-trained interrogator of many years standing. Forrester was unquestionably a top man. It pleased me to think they hadn't sent a beginner. Finally he said:

'And you haven't reached any decision on exactly where the Senator will want to go tomorrow night?'

'Not yet. He told me he'd think it over and let me know when I get to the hotel,' I laughed. 'I don't believe the man trusts even me not to tell anybody.'

Forrester frowned.

'It's really very difficult to cope with a thing like this. Any visit from a leading political figure provides enough headaches for my department. But to have someone whom we know perfectly well is going to try to evade our security precautions, well I tell you quite frankly Stevens, it's nerve-racking.'

'I can imagine.'

I tried to sound sympathetic. It wasn't hard,

I really did feel this man had a tough assignment. He sat now, staring at the carpet and thinking hard. His next question came at me sideways.

'Have you a gun, Stevens?'

I grinned.

'I'm disappointed in you, Forrester. You know all about me, who I am, where I come from, everything. You probably know the last time I put on a fresh shirt. Over here you have laws about guns. There's a licence necessary before anybody can own one. Are you trying to tell me you don't know whether or not I have a gun?'

He grinned back.

'Not exactly. I know you haven't a licence, certainly. But I also know you've had a great deal to do with guns of one kind and another. Might have picked up the habit of having one around, and not felt like breaking the habit just for the sake of an official form.'

'You must think I'm crazy,' I told him. 'You think I'd risk a business like mine by breaking one of your laws that way? No gun.'

'Very well.'

He was non-committal. He wasn't saying whether he believed me or not, merely that he'd noted what I said. From a side-pocket he drew out a folded piece of paper and handed it to me.

'Sign at the bottom. I'll have the rest filled in later.'

I unfolded the paper. It was a printed form. If I signed at the bottom I'd be making application for a firearms licence. I dug around and located a pen, signed on the dotted line, and handed the application blank back.

He looked at it, nodded, and put it away.

'What's it all about?' I asked.

'I'm taking a chance on you, Lord help me. You seem reasonably honest, and I have your service record in mind. In addition to which, you are the only candidate.' This was a joke, and I smiled politely. 'So it looks as though you have the job.'

'Job?'

'Oh come, it's fairly obvious surely? You are to see the Senator tomorrow night and take him gallivanting around town. My men will be on your tail, but there's always a nasty possibility they might lose you. If that should happen, there'll be only one person available who could do anything to help Masters if he got into a—a situation. That person will be you. You look as if you can take care of yourself, and you've seen a gun before. I'm getting you one. It'll be here in the morning.'

'Listen,' I looked concerned. 'You're not very cheerful company are you? You're suggesting there might be the kind of trouble where I'd need a gun? Count me out, brother. I'll tell the Senator my old maid aunt just flew in from Boston. Night-life is out while she's around.'

He shook his head and the penetrating eyes twinkled.

'I can't hear you speak while your knees are knocking together like that. You're overdoing it, Stevens. This little outing won't worry you in the slightest. I know too much about you, remember. Made it my business to find out before I came here with this idea. What kind of gun do you prefer, an automatic or a revolver?'

'Long as I'm hooked, and I seem to be, make it an automatic. A thirty-eight if you can.'

'I think we might manage that,' he assented. 'Now, this gun business is of course a last resort. We'll have to try to make the gun unnecessary. What I'd like you to do is get word to my people the moment you know where you're making for. Just scribble it on a piece of paper and drop it somewhere. Anywhere, once you've left the Senator's suite. My people will find it, never fear.'

That sounded like a sensible idea. Much better than all this 'lone lawman faces overwhelming odds' bit. I nodded.

'I'll do my best. Mind you, this guy is not a sleepy type. I'm going to have to be pretty slippery if I'm going to manage to write any notes without him spotting me. He doesn't walk around with his eyes closed.'

Forrester said evenly:

'I'm not asking for a guide book, Stevens. Just one word will be enough. Surely you can be that slippery?'

'I can try. Listen, are you sure any of this is a good idea?'

He elevated the grey eyebrows.

'I'm afraid I don't quite understand.'

'Tipping you off, I mean. Bentley told me that if Masters gets wind that half the O.S.S. is sitting around watching he'll likely just ditch me and go off by himself. Then you'll really have trouble.'

He inclined his immaculate head.

'That is also what I've been told. But you need have no fear on that score. My people will be discretion itself. You won't even be able to pick them out from the crowd.'

'Well, it's your business to know, I guess,' I conceded.

'Good, then it's settled.'

He got up and smoothed unnecessarily at his pants.

'I'm not going to tell you I feel better about any of this,' he told me. 'Frankly, I don't expect to get a wink of sleep until Senator Masters is safely deposited back at Idlewild. But it's good to know that you'll be trying to help us. Thank you.'

He held out a hand and I found myself shaking it. At the door I said, almost as an afterthought,

'By the way, you don't employ anybody

named Roxanne Baxter, I guess?'

He paused in the doorway and as he turned towards me his face was expressionless.

'It's a very large department, you understand. One can't possibly recall every name. Why do you ask?'

I tried to be expressionless too.

'Some day when you're glancing through the records of this enormous department, you may come across the name. If you should, give her a message. Tell her I think she owes me something, and she knows what it is. If she ever feels like paying, my 'phone number is in the book.'

The quick muscular contortion that flitted across his face could have been distant cousin to a grin.

'I will certainly remember your message in such a case.'

Then he was gone. I thought he was genuine. He looked like a man whose name would be Charles Forrester. He talked and acted like the kind of top operators on the British side I'd dealt with before. He was a gold-plated certainty to be what he said he was. That's the trouble with being one of the family. They get you so you don't trust anybody. I sighed, picked up the telephone and began to dial Grosvenor.

CHAPTER SIX

The package arrived a few minutes after eight the following morning. It was delivered by a dark-haired uncommunicative man in a brown suit. With the brown suit went highly polished black shoes and I wondered what the elegant Forrester would have had to say about that.

'Will you check the contents, Mr. Stevens? I'll wait if you don't mind.'

He didn't offer to come in. I took the package to a table, stripped off the masking tape and brown paper, took the lid off a plain cardboard box. Nestling in the cotton waste was a Smith and Wesson blue-black .38 automatic. A very nice tool indeed. Poked down at the side were two clips of cartridges. I lifted out the weapon, checked the working part. Everything moved with comforting precision. I went back to the door.

Brown Suit stood impassively in the frame.

'Everything is fine, thanks,' I told him.

He shoved a book under my nose, a blue pencil imprisoned against the cover by a thick thumb.

'Sign please.'

I would have laughed, but something in Brown Suit's appearance told me he wouldn't appreciate the joke. Looking as solemn as possible I signed for 'one package containing cardboard box. For details of contents of box, refer to Department 6'. Then I handed back the book and pencil, thanked him again and closed the door. As I swallowed the last of my coffee I thought back to my interview with Forrester the night before, and my talk on the telephone afterwards. He was the genuine article all right, and the family had known he was coming to see me. Only he wasn't just Forrester. He was Sir Charles Forrester no less, and a very big wheel indeed. The family wanted me to co-operate with him, not reveal my connection with them. My co-operation could be as complete as I liked to make it, with the main consideration that I was to decide at what point to take it by myself. The point would be reached when I considered Masters might get wise to what was going on. If that happened and the high-spirited Senator got huffy and disappeared, it would not be Forrester's fault. It would be mine. Not for the first time in my life I felt bitter towards the family. They ladled out danger and responsibility in large helpings, praise with a pepper-shaker, if they remembered, and rewards never. This Masters thing was typical. If anything went wrong somebody in the family would be responsible. Different times of the day it would be different people. Rourke sometimes maybe, other men I hadn't heard of and probably never would. If they didn't fall down it would be mine all mine once Masters and I hit the town that evening. Great.

I put the automatic and the two ammunition clips in a drawer. Then I remembered Roxanne Baxter, and the little guy who watched outside, and took them out again. The only safe place for the .38 was with me. I shoved the heavy weapon in the waist band of my pants, buttoned my jacket carefully over it. In the mirror it didn't look too bad. You might have thought a man my age ought to take more exercise, but you wouldn't be able to tell what was causing the bulge. With the slips in my side pocket I left for the office.

Some comedian had said on the radio the previous day that the heat wave was breaking up, and there should be storms by this morning, Friday. I looked up at the blue sky, felt the sudden heat as the sun hit the top of my head. By the time I made the office I was wishing I could run into that weather-man. Might be a useful work-out for the automatic before I had serious business for it.

Pat Richmond looked up quickly from her desk, appraising my appearance. I returned the compliment, and got much the best of the bargain. She was in a lemon blouse today. The cut of the shiny material was obviously intended to keep La Richmond cool. It did nothing for me in that direction, plenty in others. She caught me inspecting her and the grey eyes were amused.

'I can see you're feeling much better today,

Mr. Stevens.'

'Um? Ah, oh yes. Yes thanks, Pat. Much better. C'mon in a minute.'

She followed me into the office. I sat down behind the desk, carefully adjusting my jacket so the shining butt of the automatic didn't come into view.

'What's going on here that I ought to know about?'

It was my usual opening remark. It meant I wanted to know all about the new business that had come the way of the Personal Service since the previous morning. In a business like mine, you have to know everything. It's easy enough to let other people do the work, handle everything for you. Easy. It's also a fast road to the breadline. It's your business and if you don't show any interest in it, nobody else is going to after a while. After another while you don't have any business. I insist on knowing every detail of what's being done in the main office outside. Most of the time I don't interfere with the personal couriers, unless something comes up where I think I can offer a suggestion. Outside of that I just make mental notes of what they're all up to, then have an occasional social chat with each one, dropping in little remarks to let them know the boss is still around. It may sound kind of a sloppy routine, but it works. Everybody makes a dollar, sorry pound, and the business keeps ticking. Not just ticking either, but growing.

Pat Richmond had been a real find. Plenty of girls can slap a typewriter around, but when you land one with a shrewd business head plus a flair for handling people, you have a rare find. Pat met all these requirements, and in the seven months she'd been with me I'd already raised her salary twice. In exactly twelve minutes she had put me in touch with every development in the organisation within the past twenty-four hours. I knew what every courier was working on, where all my clients were staying at the moment and what each of them would be doing during the day. When she was through I gave her a couple of notes to type up.

'Anything in the mail?'

She told me about the stuff that would interest me, then 'Oh, and that charming man who called yesterday morning sent in a cheque for those tickets you got. Even sent a note saying he was pleased with the service.'

Rourke wouldn't forget a detail like that.

'Let me see the note, will you?'

She went out, and came back in less than a minute. The note was written on hotel paper and simply said he was glad he'd called in. Nothing more. There was no way of reading any second message into the words. The note was exactly what it seemed to be, part of Rourke's cover.

'Mr. Stevens, will you tell me something?' asked Pat.

102

'I might.'

'How did you get those seats? None of our people has been able to book for Chips and Tobacco for the last fortnight.'

I chuckled.

'Oh come on now, Pat. You know too much about this organisation as it is. The only thing I can do that you can't is to get seats for Chips and Tobacco. If I told you how to do that, you wouldn't need me at all.'

She smiled. I always enjoyed watching those red lips part over the even white teeth.

'Well that's it, Mr. Stevens. There are several items for your signature in the folder. Shall I wait?'

'No thanks. Don't want to take up your time watching me work. Couple of things in there I want to look at rather carefully. I'll buzz you when I'm through.'

She went out. I watched with regret as the door closed on her tight little rear then flipped open the folder and began to read.

The morning passed uneventfully. At twelve I called Pat in and told her I'd be going out in the afternoon. Anything that needed my attention had better be done now, as I wasn't certain whether I'd be back the rest of the day.

CHAPTER SEVEN

The cab driver pulled up in a side street at the back of the Albert Hall and looked over his shoulder.

'Dunno if you're in a hurry guvnor,' he remarked. 'I won't be able to drop you at the front door here for about another ten minutes or more. Everybody in London is queued up outside the 'All today.'

'Okay thanks. I'll walk from here.'

I paid him and got out. Half a dozen mounted police were stationed at the next corner. They would be reserves I decided, ready to be called if needed. When I turned the corner I could see where they might get that call before too long. A crowd of about forty men were lounging around on the sidewalk. They wore black shirts and pants and had armlets with a device painted on. The device wasn't a swastika but you had to look twice to be certain. I walked through this bunch. They weren't interested in me, two of them even moved out of the way to let me pass. I came to a side road, and here a procession was forming up. This was a totally different bunch from the neo-Nazis. There were several hundred of them and if it hadn't been for the banners it would have been a hard job to decide what they had in common.

There were weirds in beards, leather jackets, business suits. Women who looked like moviestars, housewives, tramps. Young men, old men, schoolboys. Typists, beatniks. You name it, this crowd could produce it. But the banners gave the answer. These were the people the newspapers and the politicians write off as cranks and nuisance-mongers. The ones who wanted to live instead of being atomised. The non-conformists who'd sooner take a chance on mushroom poisoning than the mushroom cloud. I spotted one or two famous faces, then the corner of the next building cut them off from my view.

I was nearing the main entrance to the building now. My next group was a mob of hundreds of coloured people, mostly men. Africans in the main, though there were also Indians, Malays and even an occasional Chinese. Their banners said that the Coloured Students of London remembered Little Rock and other stuff like that. Past them I hit the main stream and I began to see what the cabbie had been driving at. The road was jammed with people from one side of the street to the other. There seemed to be a vague intention, to move towards the front entrance to the Hall, but it was only vague. Many of the crowd seemed quite content to stay right where they were. Some were singing, some arguing others simply shouting encouragement towards the front of the crowd to move up.

There were bands. Thirty yards away, half a dozen kids were banging on guitars and singing their heads off. The crowd noises muffled most of the sound, which came thinly through the loaded air. Much further along was a brass band and this was having a much bigger success, measuring success by the volume of noise which reached the greatest number of people.

I tried to make progress without pushing anybody too hard. It was slow work. Here and there a mounted police officer loomed over the crowd, chatting, grinning at some of the ribald suggestions which were made. It wouldn't be exactly original for me to say I think the British police are wonderful, but the way they keep their tempers at times like that is an astonishing sight to anybody who's had experience of other police forces, other places.

With a lot of excuse me's, a few gentle shoves and an occasional elbow I was making progress of sorts through the slow-moving crowds. Somebody across the street had started singing hymns now and all around was this swelling chorus of Abide with Me. A quick check of my strap-watch told me that if I abided much longer I was going to miss the beginning of things inside. And if this circus outside was any indication of what to expect, I didn't want to be among the missing when the real fun started.

In competition with the hymn-singers another group started shouting slogans. They fooled around with two or three different ones, nobody making much headway. Then they made the hit-parade with 'Down with the Reds'. This was a success straight away, and soon hundreds of voices joined in the chant. Each word was pronounced distinctly and the whole thing was emphasised by handclapping and footstomping in time with the words. I suddenly realised a beefy red-faced man was looking at me queerly. He nudged the man next to him, who stopped shouting and joined in the looking. I realised suddenly what was annoying them. I wasn't joining in with the dirge.

Well, what about it? This was a free country, wasn't it? If I didn't want to join in with some mob, that was my business. Nobody could force old Scott Stevens to do what he didn't want to do, nossir. I knew my rights. Then I took another look at the big guy and his buddy. Before I knew it I was handclapping louder than anybody else, and shouting myself hoarse. The two men continued to stare at me. I think they were feeling disappointed, as though I'd cheated them of the chance for a little mob violence. You find people like them in any crowd, and their only reason for being there was to see what they could stir up in the way of trouble. Then I had an idea. No reason why these two should have their fun spoiled.

Next minute I planted a firm elbow in what looked like a suitable back. A glowering face turned towards me.

'Oo you shovin'?'

The front fulfilled the promise of the back. My new friend was every ounce as beefy as the one who'd been watching me.

'I wasn't meaning to shove, friend,' I said placatingly. 'I was watching those two troublemakers.'

'Eh? Making trouble? Oo?'

I nodded towards Beefy the First and his buddy. Beefy the Second looked at them carefully.

'They don't seem to think much of us,' I suggested. 'They're not joining in at all, and they don't look exactly friendly, do they?'

Beefy the Second ignored me and stuck his head between two people who were clapping away heartily. He seemed to know them.

'Gotta coupla big—'eds over here,' he shouted.

They looked. So did a few other people, sensing that something was in the air besides slogans. Beefy Two went up to Beefy One and said in a nasty tone:

'Wass up wi' you then?'

Several others murmured with approval. Beefy One wasn't going to give in so easily. By way of reply he shot out his fist suddenly, catching my champion in the middle. It didn't win him any prizes. Immediately two of the bystanders clipped Beefy the First from two different directions. I grinned happily. Two minutes earlier I might have found myself in a very ugly situation. Now I was just a guy minding his own business and wondering why the hand-clapping was dying off.

People surged away from the side of the building to see what was going on in the middle of the street. By a determined effort I managed to make it to the narrow alleyway now formed between the edge of the crowd and the side of the Hall. Now I was able to make good progress, and in a short time I'd arrived at one of the side entrances. More shoving, more elbow, and I was part of a jostling mob moving slowly up the stone steps. Inside the barrier at the top, the patient attendants inspected every admission card before letting the holder through. The man who checked mine said:

'Top of the stairs, third block on the right.'

I went up, finally located my seat and parked. Inside there was order, so far. The business of inspecting the tickets slowed down the outside crush to a steady trickle at each entrance and the place was filling rapidly, but without any commotion. The pandemonium outside was hushed to no more than a distant rumble in here.

Curiously, I looked down at the platform. There was a straight row of tables behind which were three lines of chairs, probably a hundred altogether. Framed behind the middle of the tables, and forming a centre-piece was a huge semi-circle of white-painted wood. On this was written:

ALL LOVERS OF FREEDOM
WELCOME
EDWARD P. MASTERS

At each side of this sweeping statement was a silk banner bearing the words 'Freedom Council'. Next to these came the various flags, banners and other paraphernalia of the many organisations which had banded together to fill this vast hall today.

Many of the platform delegates were already in their places. They wore the national costumes of a dozen different countries, and were all engaged in lively chatter while they waited for the arrival of the great man.

In front of the platform a brass band was pumping away at a Souza march. The whole thing reminded me strongly of the early stages of a political convention back home. There was the excitement, the feeling on all sides that something important was going to happen here today. I looked almost hopefully for signs of any drum majorettes, but that would have been going too far. The only females on view were mostly of the earnest variety.

Close by each entrance and stairway I spotted little groups of men. They weren't talking to each other, but spent the time studying the crowd. They had no uniform but they didn't need any for purposes of identification. They were the law.

At two twenty-five the last of the ticket holders were hurrying into their places. Newsreel and television cameras filled in the waiting time by taking shots of the crowd, zooming every now and then on to a well-known face. Officials scuttered around, checking watches and fussing over last-minute details. The place was heavy with smoke which hung lazily in the stifling atmosphere. Next to me a man started coughing. From the row in front came a chorus of 'Sh' and two men appeared at the side of the platform. Immediately there was silence, while they were identified. The one in front was Stavros, the other one I didn't know.

A thin cheer broke out from those nearest the platform, swelling as those further back realised the secretary of the Freedom Council was advancing towards the cluster of mikes on the middle table. Finally, practically everyone in the place was cheering or clapping or both. Stavros made it to the centre spot and stood facing the crowd, smiling broadly. Then he held up his hands for silence, and gradually the noise subsided. After it was quiet he stood motionless, staring out into the vast amphitheatre. There was no smile now, and as the last distant handclap faded away Stavros

111

suddenly flung wide his arms, like a man welcoming home a long-lost son.

'The Freedom Council,' he roared.

Just like that. A tremendous wave of feeling ran through the crowd.

They cheered, they clapped. They stood up and stamped their feet on the floor. Some wept, and they weren't all women. The man was electric, standing there on the platform holding out his arms to every individual in the place. I could even get the feeling myself, and I was just an interloper. These were the real lovers of freedom, the ones I'd sneered at mentally a few minutes earlier. These were the people who knew the real meaning of freedom, these one time refugees from prison-camps, labour battalions and the political prisons. They knew just what it was they were against, and why. Looking round at them now, watching their faces, seeing their expressions I could begin to feel a little less annoyed about Stavros' attitude when I'd talked with him the day before.

He was motioning them to be silent again.

'Free men and free women—' he began, and another minor commotion broke out, but this time he flagged them down quickly, '—I am not here to make a speech, I am not going to delay that great moment for which you are all waiting. We of the Freedom Council have had many great moments, but none which has brought us the same pleasure which we feel today. Are feeling at this very moment. The man who is now to address you has been our friend for many years, but this is the first occasion on which it has been our good fortune to welcome him in person. You all know the man I am speaking of. He is a citizen of that great free country across the ocean, the United States of America.' Prolonged cheers 'He is a man who is dedicated to the same cause which has brought us together, a tireless fighter for freedom,' More cheers. 'He is the one man who can be relied on to see that the Western Powers do not for a moment forget the enemy that is within our gates.'

Stavros dropped his voice as he said the last part, eyes moving ceaselessly through the crowd. On the word 'enemy' he almost spat out the syllables. He had them now. The hysteria was gone, the mob-feeling. Now he was crouched forward slightly over the bunched microphones, talking personally to every man and woman in the place. And he had them, there was no doubt about that.

'This man,' he said softly, Is the beacon of our cause.'

Now he stood up straight.

'Let him hear your voices now,' he commanded, flinging out an arm to point dramatically at the side of the platform. 'United States Senator, Edward P. —'

He must have mentioned Masters last name, but it was lost in the deafening roar that went up from the packed assembly. Masters didn't forget his stagecraft. He delayed his entrance till the din reached full volume. Then, quite suddenly, he stepped into view. I had to admit he made an impressive figure as he strode slowly and confidently towards the waiting Stavros. The privileged people on the platform stood to a man, clapping and cheering with the best.

Stavros clasped the senator's outstretched hand and the two men stood smiling at each other. This gave second wind to the audience, who let go with their appreciation in positive fashion. Stavros sat down, and Masters turned full-face to the crowd. This was no travelling salesman now. I knew there'd be no harem girls on this man's braces. This was the big-time pro politician, the public figure. He stood and waited to be heard.

'Friends—'

And that was all he said.

From the third row a shot rang out. Behind Masters and to his right, one of the platform delegates screamed, got up from his chair and held out a hand as if to support himself. Then he crashed forward across the tables, a couple of feet from where Masters stood. The gunman was standing, a wild figure of a man with a heavy-calibre revolver in his hand. He pointed the gun at Masters a second time. After that everything happened in a flash. Stavros tried to jump in front of Masters, but he wouldn't let him. The man next to the killer pushed against him, deflecting the gun. All around, the crowd were lashing out at the assassin. He went down quickly under a heap of struggling, kicking men. Police were moving fast to the spot from half-a-dozen directions. On the platform, anxious people were bent over the prostrate delegate who'd been hit. Things became confused. So many people were on the move now down in the body of the hall that it was impossible to get a clear picture of what was going on. I felt useless sitting where I was, but there was nothing I could contribute which would be of any real help. At least by staying put, I was making one less to block the jammed gangway. Nearly everybody else in the place seemed to think he could do some good by adding to the confusion. Masters' confident voice boomed suddenly:

'My friends, I beg you to return to your seats. There has been a tragic incident here, and it is our duty to keep calm and allow the proper authorities to deal with the matter.'

Then he sat down, picked up a tumbler of water from in front of him and sipped at it.

I don't know whether it was the voice, the words, or the water trick. What I do know is that within five minutes chaos had been reduced to mere confusion, with a lot of people back in their seats and the rest no longer moving, but scattered around in bunches chattering excitedly, uncertain what to do next.

Every few seconds somebody would walk on to the platform, talk urgently with Masters and Stavros, then go off again. These were the bulletin men, keeping the main speakers informed about what was going on offstage. That was something I would have given a lot to know. The man in the next seat nudged me suddenly. I turned to him and he pointed to the end of the row. A man stood there, beckoning me. I'd never seen him before but I thought I recognised the type. I nodded and got up. Nobody paid any attention to one more eager beaver who couldn't keep his seat during a time of excitement. The man didn't wait for me to join him. Instead, once he saw I'd started to move, he went up the aisle stairs and paused at the top.

I trod on my last foot, made it to the gangway and went up the stairs. His face was devoid of expression as he watched me climb towards him. I had a momentary twinge of uneasiness. Suppose somebody had found out what I was doing, who I was working for? I wasn't much of a figure, but maybe I had a nuisance value. Suppose they thought they'd be better off without that extra nuisance? The crowded place didn't offer any comfort. An outfit which had just attempted to eliminate a United States Senator, in front of thousands of people, wouldn't even rate it as a workout to knock off one part-worn out-of-practice

Government agent. The man at the top looked huge as I headed up the stairs. I told myself to get with it, there couldn't be anything to worry about. Just the same I was conscious of relief when he said:

'Mr. Stevens? Come with me please.'

He turned to go, but I caught at his sleeve.

'Hold on, brother. Why should I go with you, and where are we going?'

He took a card from his pocket. It said he was an inspector of the Metropolitan Police, and I'd seen enough like it to know it was the McCoy.

'If you don't mind, sir. We are rather busy just now.'

The words were polite, but this guy was telling me to stop fooling around. I went with him.

In London it seemed to be Throw-the-manager-out-of-his-office Week. This one was bigger than the one where I'd spent so many happy moments at the Skyroof Hotel, but that only meant space for more cops. Last night there were two, today there were eight, plus a lot of to-ing and fro-ing as others came in to make reports and get instructions. The man in charge, a grizzled sixty-year-old, was a stranger. The man sitting by the window was Forrester.

My escort led me up to the desk and we stood waiting while crisp orders were issued to the two men who faced the top man. They nodded and went out. We moved into their places. The seated man was almost entirely bald, except for a ring of curly white hair which fringed his pate almost like a monk's. The resemblance ended there. No monk had a right to all the shrewd knowledge that looked out of the pale grey eyes.

'What's this?' he barked at the inspector.

'Mr. Stevens, sir,' replied my man.

Forrester hadn't taken any notice of me up to now. He looked across and nodded.

'Oh yes, thanks Inspector. Check the front entrance please. Let me know if the reinforcements from Central are not here in the next four minutes.'

'Right sir.'

The inspector went out. The other men in the room looked at me curiously. Forrester said:

'Like to have this conversation between ourselves, if you don't mind, Tom.'

'Certainly, Sir Charles.'

Tom told the others to clear out. When the door was closed Forrester spoke again.

'This is Chief Superintendent Harker, Stevens.'

We said hallo, and since nobody had thought to ask me I got a chair and brought it up to the desk.

'What can I do for you gentlemen?' I wanted to know.

'You saw what happened just now?'

demanded Forrester.

'Had a good view. Who was the man who got shot?'

'His name was Lieven, a prominent figure in this movement from Western Germany,' replied Harker.

I grimaced.

'Is he dead?'

Forrester shook his head.

'Not yet. The doctor who carried out the initial examination said it was unlikely he'd live more than a few hours. You understand that is confidential, of course.'

'Of course,' I agreed. 'Well, short of actually killing Masters, this guy couldn't have picked a worse subject from your point of view could he? I mean it's going to be kind of embarrassing for the boys in the striped pants over there isn't it?'

Forrester nodded.

'Yes. But it would have been just as embarrassing somewhere else whoever on that platform was killed. Every man on it is a leading figure in his own country. Lieven was the unlucky one, that's all.'

'I see. This guy who did it, has he talked at all?'

Harker shrugged.

'Nothing coherent, the people in there didn't exactly treat him like a long-lost brother. He has a fractured leg, four fractured ribs, possibly five. His face has been smashed to a pulp and there are multiple internal injuries where he was stamped on.' He sighed heavily. 'In fact he'll be unfit for questioning probably for several days.'

So by the time they were able to get anything from the gunman, always supposing they got anything at all, it would be too late to be of any value in looking after Masters.

'Any leads as to who the guy is?'

Harker held up three bullets.

'The total contents of his pockets,' he said flatly. 'Also, there were no maker's labels on any of his clothes and no laundry marks on his linen.'

'Sounds like a pro,' I admitted. 'Still, it doesn't make sense to me. You send out a man to do a job as important as this, you don't expect sloppy work. How do you suppose he came to miss?'

It was Forrester's turn to reply.

'We can't be absolutely certain yet, but we'll know in a few hours. My theory is this. During the war there was an arms factory in Germany which was producing automatic hand weapons, including revolvers. Some resistance people got employed there, one of them a munitions expert. He managed to tamper with the rifling of the barrels, in such a way that they all fired high right. The plant turned out almost a quarter of a million of these revolvers before they found out what was going on. You see, we had another man on the test range in the same factory. It was a beautiful idea and it worked like a charm. Until the Gestapo caught up with them, of course.'

'Uh huh. And you think it's likely the gun this man used today was one of those from that plant?'

Forrester nodded.

'I think it's a good bet, yes. They were sent out in quantities to every theatre of war. Must be scattered all over the world by now. It's just a theory of course. But I agree with you that for a man to be detailed for an important mission like today's, he would have to be an expert shot. I can't believe there could be anything wrong with his markmanship. Therefore we are only left with the weapon.'

I thought it was a long shot but I wasn't there to argue.

'Don't think I'm not interested in what you're telling me Sir Charles, but there's one thing I don't get. Why bring me in here and toss me all this information? It's none of my business.'

That seemed to meet with more approval from the chief superintendent than anything I'd said so far. A small grunt of agreement escaped from him before he could check it. Immediately, he began to burn a dull red around the throat. Forrester grinned quickly.

'Well, you seemed to strike a chord with Harker here that time, Stevens. Still, I don't think I've told you very much that we won't release to the press in any case. In due time, that is. Naturally you will keep it under your hat.'

He waited for my nod, then went on.

'Actually, you're quite right. There is something else. A development since we had our little talk last night. Not altogether unexpected. During the small hours a freighter arrived in the Port of London. She wasn't scheduled, and the story is that she has engine trouble and had to dock here instead of finishing her journey.'

'And where would the journey have finished if she hadn't had this engine trouble?' I queried.

'Helsinki,' he replied softly.

I didn't get it. For a moment I stood there trying to look intelligent but nothing came out.

'All right,' I conceded, 'I know where Helsinki is but it doesn't get me any further. You mean you think maybe this gunman was going to try to make it to the boat, once he killed Masters?'

Forrester shook his head. Harker sighed gently.

'Think man, think,' he remonstrated. 'You don't suppose anybody thought for a moment that man would get away from the Albert Hall, after doing what he did? Whoever sent him in there knew then it was certain death. If the crowd didn't kill him, the law would in the end. You saw what happened, it was a miracle we got him away from that mob in one piece. No, nobody expected him to get out. That much is certain.'

'That sounds O.K. So why the boat?'

'We can only guess, Stevens,' chipped in Forrester. 'These people are thorough, that much we know for certain. Now, supposing they reasoned this way. Try for an assassination at the rally. If it doesn't come off, have another try somewhere else. Or even at something else.'

'Something like what?'

'Like kidnapping. Take Masters back to— wherever they take him back to—then fill him full of drugs, make him denounce the United States, all the Western alliance. It's been done before.'

I shook my head slowly.

'I don't buy that, necessarily. Seems to me if I had a scheme like that, I'd make that the number one try. Yeah, that's what I'd do. I'd go for the snatch as the main event, not as a second feature. Then, if something was going wrong, then I'd kill him. It's the wrong way round, the way you're putting it up. No.'

To my surprise, Forrester nodded in agreement.

'Good reasoning. I think I agree with that.'

This time I really gave up.

'All right, you lost me. Tell me slowly, will you? I don't seem to be at my best this afternoon.'

'Don't forget I'm still guessing,' he reminded me. 'Let's ignore the gunman. He tried, he failed and now his whole future in this life consists of getting himself thoroughly fit for the hangman. As a figure he has already ceased to exist. Right?'

'Right.'

'Now let's take the ship. Her name is the Latyva, by the way. L-a-t-y-v-a. Better remember it. The ship is very much alive, and anchored in London at this moment. She can't be ignored. In fact she's the one tangible thing on which we can concentrate. Why is she here? To send gunmen swarming over the side? Hardly likely. She only arrived last night, and if you're going to kill somebody, somebody important, you lay the whole thing on well in advance. You don't rely on some last-minute hasty arrangements. Agreed?'

'I guess so.'

'All right. What else can she be doing here. Ships carry people. They either take them to a place, or from it. We've agreed we don't think she's brought anyone. Who then, is she going to take away? A gunman who's been planted well in advance? Unlikely. Anybody who tries to kill the senator, successful or not, is absolutely certain to be caught. So what remains? It has to be the senator himself who'll be on that ship when she enters Helsinki. If indeed that's where she's headed.'

Forrester had a very persuasive way of

talking, but even allowing for that he made a lot of sense. Grudgingly, I said: 'The way you tell it, there's no other explanation.'

His eyes twinkled.

'Not at all, my boy. There may be others. Lots of others. But we haven't time for them. We have to work in the dark and time is our enemy. These people know exactly what they're going to do. All we can do is sit around guessing, and hoping one of those guesses will be near the mark.'

I made one last try with my assassin.

'Even if you're right, it's all based on ignoring what happened just now in there.'

'Yes. And I think we can. I think that was a sideshow. I've come up against these people in many places. China, Poland, Africa. Even the United States.' He grinned to show there was no offence in the words. 'They are not sloppy. You can say many things against their work. They are unimaginative, crude even. They lack invention, if any small detail comes unstuck, they don't seem able to improvise an alternative at short notice. But they are not sloppy. If they send a man out to shoot somebody, he would not receive a defective weapon. No, it's my view that man was either a lone wolf, or he represented some minor group of extremists. Our friends have not yet made their move.'

I nodded.

'O.K. I think you sold me. Half an hour

after I walk out of here I'll think of a dozen questions. But right now, I'm sold.'

'Good.' Forrester seemed satisfied. 'Now, if we are going to assume that I'm right about the S.S. *Latyva,* you will understand what I'm going to say next. I know you're not in a position to tell me about where you're heading tonight because you don't know. You are going to get a message to us as soon as you find out and that's perfectly satisfactory as far as it goes. But now there's a snag. The *Latyva.* If you find Masters heading anywhere near the area of the docks, you are to stop him. I don't care what you do, but you've got to stop him. Anything may go wrong. You may give our people the slip. I've talked to the Washington boys and I know how good our friend Masters can be at shaking off policemen. So you could just possibly be the only one near him. And if that happens, you have got to stop him from going too near the docks.'

Forrester came up close and stared into my face.

'Even if you have to put a bullet in his arm, or better still his leg. You will stop him, Stevens.'

I felt uncomfortable.

'What the hell,' I muttered. 'This whole thing is ridiculous. I have a good mind to go and tell Masters to get another boy.'

'But there isn't another boy,' objected Forrester. 'It's either you go with him, or he'll wander away and get lost by himself. You know that already.'

'So I know it. It doesn't make me feel one damned bit better,' I said irritably. 'It seems to me that if you hotshots from London and Washington can't manage to look after this guy between you, it's asking a hell of a lot of an ordinary private joe to take it on.'

'I agree,' returned Forrester smoothly. 'Candidly, I think the entire business is a disgrace. I've told my superiors what I think about it. The point is if your man Masters hadn't got this streak of unpleasantness in him, none of this would arise. What your government is thinking of letting him make this trip, is beyond me.'

'Really? Well, I can probably help you there. If my people tried to stop a man like Ed Masters going just where he pleases, they'd find themselves up against a barrage of public opinion that would stink up every corridor in Washington.'

He nodded affably.

'That is my understanding, too. So he had to come, and being what he is, he has to go where he's going tonight. And being what you are, you're going to go with him and try to keep him out of trouble. Aren't you?'

I nodded back without warmth.

'Guess I am.'

'That all then, Sir Charles?' queried Harker. 'I really ought to be keeping in touch with my men outside.'

'Thank you, Chief Superintendent. I think we have just about finished.'

I got up to go. Then a thought struck me.

'By the way, this stuff about the *Latyva*. You didn't have to call me in here to tell me all that. You could have done it at my office or my apartment. Somewhere more private.'

'Yes, I could,' agreed Forrester. 'But I thought this way was better. The people we're up against must have agents swarming round the hall like flies. Your call to this office will have been noted by half-a-dozen at least. You were nowhere near the gunman or the platform, they'll know that. So you must have some connection with us, they'll surmise.'

I objected.

'Well that ought to decrease my value about fifty per cent. I should imagine.'

'Not at all. You see, if they try anything on the senator tonight they'll know you're not just a casual companion. They'll know you're with us. So if you should feel any last-minute temptation to decide the whole thing is none of your business, you'll be wasting your time. They will know they have to take care of you in any case. Now you know where they stand, it will give you a clearer picture of where you stand.'

I resisted an impulse to plant a fist in that urbane face. He had me.

'Yes,' I said grimly. 'Now it isn't just me

doing my best to save Masters. It's me or them. That's the message isn't it?'

He shrugged and pursed his lips.

'Good luck Stevens.'

'Thanks.'

I tried to make it sound like an insult as I slammed out. As I left the building an elderly man hurried past me inside. I thought the strained and anxious face was familiar, and certainly the boys with the cameras were giving him plenty of action. So he had to be important. Probably, I reflected with relish, important enough to make Forrester squirm at the forthcoming interview.

I felt almost cheerful again.

CHAPTER EIGHT

I went back to the office but found I couldn't get my mind concentrated on the work. After about thirty minutes I gave it up and went home. It was time I called the Grosvenor boys anyway. By now they'd have had time to mull over the Albert Hall thing, and decide what they wanted me to do. My reception, judged by previous experience, was almost excited.

'Jeremy?' intoned the flat voice. 'You took your time about calling.'

'Wanted to give you people a chance to decide whether you wanted to change my instructions,' I suggested hopefully.

'Wait.'

I waited. As I stood holding the silent 'phone I reflected, not for the first time, that the man at the other end could have done with a re-read on 'Confidence and How to Inspire It'. A muffled noise told me he was coming back on the line. Without preamble he said:

'No change. Just carry on.'

'Do you want me to report on what happened at the Albert Hall?'

'No. We know all about it,' he told me discouragingly.

And that was that. Here I was stuck with a whole empty evening to fill, and the gloomy prospect of my big night out with Clay-Pigeon Masters at the end of it. The only sensible thing to do seemed to be to catch a couple of hours' sleep. No telling what time of night I'd be through with the fun-assignment.

I stretched out on the bed, kicking my shoes off. One habit had been instilled into me during early training for this kind of work. Sleep is a necessity if you need your mind alert and your body active. You never know when you'll get your next full ration, so any opportunity that presents itself, you conk off. Was a time I could do it standing if I had to, as long as there was something to lean against.

Within two minutes I was asleep, conscious as I drifted off of a feeling of self-satisfaction that I could still summon up the old habit at will.

A vital sequel to the ability to fall asleep any place any time, is the related ability to come awake instantly. Every faculty alert, every sense operating at one hundred per cent efficiency.

As I mumbled and stretched my way out of what seemed like a woolly blanket pulled tightly round my mind, I reflected how odd it was that I could still doze off as efficiently as ever, and yet the waking-up bit eluded me. Eluded me, I may say, considerably. I sat up yawning and scratching, trying to remember where I was, and why I should be waking up. And it didn't help with my thinking to have that racket going on in my ears. Racket? What kind of a racket? A buzzer. Yes, definitely a buzzer. Two, or possibly three of my faculties were now alert, or thereabouts, and several senses were approaching the fifty per cent efficiency mark. I even began to wonder whether perhaps there was anything significant about the buzzer. From there it was only a short step to the truth. It was the door-buzzer. The years of early training had now asserted themselves. Within three minutes of waking up, I knew the cause. Somebody was at the door.

I rolled wearily off the bed, peeked in the mirror to straighten my tie then went to the door.

Pat Richmond stood outside, anxiety plain

on her face.

'Mr. Stevens, are you all right?'

I nodded.

'I'm all right Pat. Why wouldn't I be?'

'Well—'

She stood there, undecided about whether to hold this conversation from the hall, or whether there was a chance she might be asked inside.

'Say, I'm sorry,' I said quickly. 'C'mon in.'

She came on in and I closed the door.

'Come and sit down,' I invited. 'Can I get you something, a drink maybe?'

'Er—oh—no thank you, Mr. Stevens.'

Now that she was in, she didn't seem too happy about it. I wondered whether she thought—but, it couldn't be that. I'd had plenty of opportunities to try playing footsie with this girl, and I hadn't ever attempted it. Not that it wouldn't be a pleasure, but good secretaries are like uranium mines in London. You get one, you hang on to her. Figuratively.

So it wasn't that. Something else then. I sat down in the opposite chair and lit a cigarette. The idea was to look composed and unruffled, until I crossed one knee over the other and found I wasn't wearing any shoes.

'What's this all about, Pat?'

She smiled fleetingly.

'Seems silly now. Now that I'm here, talking to you. Just my foolish imagination, I expect.'

I'd never seen any signs of foolishness about

Pat Richmond. Trying not to look too eager, I prompted.

'Well, whatever it was, it seemed real enough to bring you here. Why not tell me the story?'

'All right,' she nodded. 'But you're not to laugh, and if it's all my imagination, you'll have to promise not to pull my leg about it in the office.'

'Very well,' I agreed. 'Now.'

She pressed her hands together, and began.

'I've been working for you now a little over seven months. Worked close beside you a good deal of the time, and for a woman that can be a very revealing situation. You get to know a man, know his habits, his likes and dislikes.'

'The same goes both ways,' I reminded her.

'True. Now, you've always had a great regard for the detail work in the office. Some bosses just leave things to run themselves, others are interested in the smallest detail. You come under the second heading.'

I already knew that, but felt I ought to nod.

'The past couple of days you haven't been concentrating at all. I took no notice of the first two or three bits of office routine you ignored. Well,' she qualified, 'that isn't exactly true. I did notice, but what I meant was I didn't regard it as anything serious. I thought perhaps the heat was beginning to get you down too, or perhaps you had something on your mind.'

133

She waited to see if I had anything to offer on that.

'But now you think differently?'

'Yes. In the past forty-eight hours you've been missing from your desk more than half the time. I've never known you do anything like it before. No, let me finish.'

She saw I was about to butt in, so she went on quickly.

'By itself, that was curious. But it could be explained. Then there was that business yesterday morning when I found you unconscious on the floor. That's what it was, wasn't it? You weren't drunk or unwell at all.'

The question was rhetorical, and again she hurried on with her case-history.

'This morning you arrived at the office at a reasonable time. You seemed quite attentive to business. For a few moments I began to think I'd been letting my imagination get the better of me. That was before I saw the gun.'

She looked directly into my face, to see whether I was going to try to deny it. I hedged.

'Gun?'

'You had a gun stuck inside the top of your trousers. You'd pulled your jacket round it very carefully; but when you leaned down to open the bottom drawer at the side of your desk the jacket pulled away.'

I ground out the last of the cigarette.

'Go on,' I told her.

'You gave yourself the afternoon off. When

I left the office I bought my usual late edition newspaper. Here it is.'

She opened her capacious handbag, withdrew a crumpled copy of the *Evening Call* and handed it to me. The headline was about the murder of the man Lieven. There were three pictures on the front page. One was a distance shot of the crowds milling round the entrance before the meeting began. One was of Lieven, smiling and waving as he'd arrived at London Airport the previous day. The third picture was headed 'Cabinet Minister hurries to scene'. It was the worried man who'd brushed past me at the entrance to the Albert Hall. No wonder his face had seemed familiar. There was a good clear shot of his profile. And, standing sideways to the camera, and in the background but clearly recognisable, was guess-who. I folded the paper, laid it on the chair beside me.

'All right. I went to a meeting. What about it?'

'Please,' she begged. 'Don't talk to me as though I were a child. On top of everything else, this is too much of a coincidence.'

She stabbed a forefinger towards the newspaper. I thought I'd try to bluff my way out. Speaking in my most reasonable manner I said:

'Look Pat, we'll take this over from the top. You're making altogether too much out of this. In fact there isn't really any "this". Consider what you've got. You're right about the heat, it has been getting to me a little. I've had headaches, and I don't seem able to rouse myself to take any interest in things. Night before last I passed out, and it must have been from some form of heat exhaustion or something like it. As for the gun, well you make me feel pretty silly telling you this, but it was a present for the son of a friend of mine. It was in a box when I bought it, but I—' I tried to look sheepish '—Well if you must know, I thought it would give the kid a lift if I pulled it out of my waistband. You know, sort of Al Capone stuff. You're making me feel pretty silly, telling you this.'

I smiled engagingly, or so I hoped. The expression on her face encouraged me to think I was going to get away with it. She pursed her lips and asked:

'What about the meeting this afternoon, where a man just chanced to be murdered?'

'That's the weakest part of your whole fabric,' I assured her. 'It was a public meeting, there were thousands of us there.'

'I see.'

Pat nodded, as if she understood it all now.

'And you were really just one of thousands there?' she questioned. 'Just attended the meeting like any other member of the public?'

I hunched my shoulders and grinned.

''F'raid so, Pat. Sorry to knock out your fascinating plot, but I'm afraid it hasn't any bones.'

'You're a very inventive man.' There was something like admiration in her tone. 'I ahnost believed all that rubbish for a moment. But it won't do.'

I decided to become severe.

'Now look Pat, this has gone on long enough. I've told you—'

'Oh yes, you've told me,' she interrupted. 'You've told me a very plausible story. Only it isn't true.'

I was reasonable again, humouring the girl, trying to understand.

'Well tell me, what it is you question?'

She shook her head.

'Not me. Scotland Yard. They are the people who don't believe you. Not according to the paper.'

'Paper?'

'Yes. The report states that no one was allowed to leave the hall for more than an hour after the shooting. The Minister was there within thirty minutes. As he arrived, you were leaving. Thirty minutes before anybody else.'

'Oh come on,' I scoffed. 'This story was thrown together anyhow, to get it in the late editions—'

I broke off as she wagged her head firmly from side to side. 'No Scott, it won't work. The news on the radio gave exactly the same account.'

Damn. Damn everything. This girl had me all snarled up. For the life of me I couldn't see what logical explanation I could give her now. I hadn't missed the fact that she'd used my first name, either. She'd never done that before.

'All right, if you must know. I'm an anarchist. A foreign power paid me to blow up the Houses of Parliament. That's what I was doing at the Albert Hall this afternoon. I thought it was the House of Commons. Then, when I found out I had the address wrong, I got excited and shot Lieven. Satisfied? Anyway, what the hell business is it of yours?'

She smiled briefly, but there were tiny lines of worry around the grey eyes. When she spoke, her voice was soft and she was looking at the floor, not at me.

'No, I am not satisfied in the least. I think you're in trouble of some kind, serious trouble. As to what business it is of mine, this is the damnedest way to have it happen, but I'll tell you. Anything to do with you is my business, because—because I love you. Now it's my turn to say, "are you satisfied?"'

'Oh.'

It was not a brilliant rejoinder. I wasn't feeling brilliant. Flabbergasted would have been nearer the truth. Pat Richmond. The cool blonde, the super-efficient office machine, in love. And with me. Ordinarily I'm quick with the words, but at that moment there seemed to be only one left in my vocabulary. So I said it again.

'Oh.'

Pat chuckled at my discomfiture, but was immediately serious again.

'You don't look exactly ecstatic about it, but I didn't expect you to. The point is, you wanted to know why it was my business. Well, I've told you.' She spoke briskly, as though trying to gloss over that part of it. 'So now you know where I stand. I know you're in some kind of serious trouble. I don't care what it is, don't even want to know, unless you choose to tell me. What I'm saying is please, please let me help. There must be something I can do. Anything.'

'Pat, I—I don't know what to say,' I mumbled.

'If you mean about the state of affairs between you and me, you can ignore that. Just leave it that. I feel I've a right to be here, to help. Please don't send me away.'

I got up. My mind was racing now, and a drink would help. Aside from which, a little work with the bottles would give me a thinking space.

'I'm going to have a drink,' I announced. 'Are you sure I can't get you something?'

'Changed my mind. Is there a dry sherry?'

'There is.'

She sat there, calm and beautiful, while I set about sorting out glasses. To anybody else she would simply have been a delectable blonde. To me she was that too, but also a king-size headache. If I'd had a straightforward problem I'd have known what to do about it. If all I'd had to worry about was the welfare of Senator Masters it would have been easy. But that was only part of the story. The Masters episode would last only a couple more days at most. After that I'd be back to normal again, a man with a business to look after and that was what made Pat Richmond so important. Not that she was indispensable, I wasn't dumb enough to let anybody in the Personal Service get to that stage. But she was important, just the same. If I ever had to stay out on some assignment for two or three days, I always knew the Service was operating smoothly, not a file-tray out of place. That was all Pat's doing, and it would be a major upset to me if I had to try replacing her. The personal bit we could get around to later. Right now I had the option of telling this girl some highly secret information, or of throwing her out and my smooth-running organisation with her. Great.

'You'd never make a barman,' she said gently.

I was taking too long over the drinks, and Pat was reminding me she was there. As though I could forget it.

'Try this.'

I held out the slim-stemmed glass and she sipped.

'M'm. Delicious. What's that?'

'Scotch,' I replied, downing half of it.

This was the time. I sat down again and dived off.

'Pat,' I began seriously, 'I don't know how you worked all this out, but yes, I am in a little trouble.'

She nodded.

'Naturally. How little?'

'Well,' I admitted, making a wry face, 'Not as little as I'd like. After tonight I'll know for sure whether it really is just a little or whether it's a whole stinking mess.'

She sipped at the amber liquid.

'Tonight?' she prompted.

'Yes. I have to see some people, talk with them. Afterwards I'll know how bad it is.'

'Are you going to tell me about it?'

The enquiry was casual, but the grey eyes were alive with eager concern. Now I'd have to ham it up.

'Did you ever stop to think how little you know about me, Pat?'

'I know enough,' she replied softly.

That wasn't the direction I wanted to travel. Not at all.

'I haven't been over here all that long. Little over a year. I had this notion to set up the Personal Service, see how it worked out. Well, it worked out, as you know. I make a fair amount of money, you could say I'm a success. It wasn't always like that.'

141

I let my face cloud over, and didn't miss the quick flicker of sympathy in her eyes.

'One of the reasons I came to England was to get away from—certain things. I needed a clean start and this seemed the ideal solution. Now, something's come up, something that goes back a long time.'

I left her hanging while I fooled around lighting a fresh cigarette. Through the blue haze I looked at her seriously.

'Just now you said you loved me. Was that on the level?'

'You know you don't need to ask me that,' she returned.

I studied her face.

'No,' I admitted. 'No, I needn't have asked. If you love someone you trust them. Right?'

'You know the answer to that, too.'

'Then trust me. Right now, there isn't a thing you can do to help. It isn't that I wouldn't let you, or ask even. Believe me, there's nothing. What's going to happen tonight is between me and these people.'

'I see.' She twiddled the slender glass around in her hand. 'And after tonight, what then?'

I shrugged.

'Quien sabe? Maybe it'll turn out to be nothing, or at least nothing to really worry about.'

'What if it doesn't?' she insisted. 'Will you let me help then.'

142

'Honey if it turns out as bad as it could, I'll need all the help I can get. Yours especially.'

She smiled gratefully.

'Thank you for that, at least. This business tonight, could it be dangerous? And before you answer, remember I saw the gun.'

I shook my head.

'Tonight, no. Yes, you saw a gun and yes, I could be needing it. But not tonight.'

'I think I see what you mean. If everything goes well tonight the gun will have been an unnecessary precaution. If things go the other way, the bad way, that's when you'll need it.'

I chuckled, and the chuckle was genuine.

'I'm not laughing at your reasoning, Pat. You're dead on target there. What's amusing me is the calm way you sit there talking about big trouble, and guns and everything. Kind of incongruous. I'll bet you never saw anything more deadly than a slingshot in your whole life. Doesn't it occur to you that you oughtn't to be here talking so calmly? That where you ought to be is down at the nearest police station, telling all this to the law?'

She smoothed at the ash-blonde head, chastising an imaginary stray hair.

'Oh yes, I thought about that, too. But there was a snag to that. I soon realised I'd no idea which side of the law this trouble might place you.'

She said that quietly, and the words were far from casual. For her the law wasn't something you played ducks and drakes with. You lived by it, respected it, regulated your whole life to it. I knew what it must be costing her to say that and mean it.

'And you don't care?'

I made it a question. She lifted her troubled face to stare at me levelly.

'Oh yes I do. I care. But it won't make any difference if you need me.'

I felt like a heel, but what could I do? There were only two other alternatives open to me, each of them out of the question. But her last statement got to me.

'I'll never forget you said that, honey.' I meant it.

'Anyway let's not get gloomy. Not tonight. In a little while now this whole business will be cleared up, and tomorrow at the office I'll tell you all about it, and we'll probably have a good laugh.'

The blonde head wagged a negative.

'Not tomorrow, Scott. Tonight. You surely don't think I'll be able to sleep until I know?'

'Well,' I hedged. 'I'm not expecting to be through with these people until pretty late.'

'Tonight,' she said definitely. 'I don't care if it's four in the morning. I'll be waiting.'

I gave in.

'Sure. Tonight. I have your home number. I'll call you the moment I'm through.'

Her head was on the move again.

'And tell me some yarn to keep me from

worrying? Oh no you don't. You come to my flat where I can look you in the face while you tell me. That way I'll be satisfied.'

It was the least I could do. I realised with surprise that I didn't even have a note at home of her address. She made me write it down, then got up to leave.

'I'll go through hell till I see you, Scott.'

Her lip trembled and there was an extra brightness to her eyes. Awkwardly I patted her on the shoulder.

'It's going to be all right,' I assured her. 'Trust me.'

We were only a few inches apart. Suddenly she leaned forward and kissed me quickly on the mouth.

'For luck,' she whispered.

Then she was gone.

My mind was a strange jumble of thoughts. I'd been lucky tonight. In many ways. A look at the clock told me it was time to empty my mind of any thoughts not connected with the safety and welfare of one Senator Edward P. Masters. Not to mention one Scott Stevens.

I hoped the luck wouldn't run out.

CHAPTER NINE

Skyroof Hotel at ten-forty that evening. Masters had said he'd want to leave around eleven, and by the time I'd been through the security rigmarole I'd probably have used up those twenty minutes. The best-dressed doorkeeper in the business looked me over carefully and was not impressed with what he saw. The kind of places Masters wanted to visit were not used to the clientele wearing two-hundred dollar suits. That was a guaranteed way to attract attention, and attention was one thing we could do without. The evening was hot and sultry, so I'd settled for a faded check shirt and nondescript dark pants. Over this assembly I'd pulled a brown sloppy sweater. Very sloppy, sloppy enough to bag all round my middle, in a way that the bulk of the .38 didn't show through. It was tucked inside the top of my pants and I wouldn't say it was exactly comfortable. But comforting, definitely.

The doorkeeper didn't open the door but came up close and peered inside as I went through. I didn't need to be much of a detective to know he was waiting to give me a fast exit if anybody in there thought it was necessary. The same smooth character was at his perch behind the reception desk. He was better trained than the doorkeeper, didn't even sneer. For all he knew I could be one of these eccentric millionaires.

'Good evening sir,' he greeted deferentially.

'Good evening,' I returned. 'Calling to see Senator Masters. The name is Stevens. I was here last night, remember?'

He didn't remember, but you'd never have known.

'Of course sir. These gentlemen will attend to you.'

I was conscious there were people behind me. Turning I met the eyes of the two watchdogs of the previous evening.

'Hallo boys. It's me again.'

'Evening Mr. Stevens,' said one.

The other merely nodded.

'You can find your own way up can't you Mr. Stevens?' the first one asked.

'No third degree tonight?'

They smiled thin tired smiles and watched me all the way into the elevator. At twelve I pushed the button and the doors slid smoothly open. Two more men were standing looking at me.

'Mr. Stevens?'

'I was on the first floor,' I pointed out.

'This way, if you please.'

One led the way, the other one fell in behind me. When we arrived at room forty-one, the leader rapped on the door. We had the Boris Karloff noises again from inside, the rasping chain and sliding bolt. The man Thomson peered out, immediately opening the door when he saw me.

'Mr. Stevens,' he greeted. 'You're early.'

'Well, you know what they say,' I replied, as I went past him.

Bentley had heard the door being opened and was now standing waiting for me, deep lines of worry etched across his face. Without preamble he said, quietly but fiercely.

'Try to talk the fool out of this, will you? You know what happened this afternoon in front of thousands of people. With only you to look after him the man is as good as dead.'

He wasn't knocking me personally. What he meant was it was more than one man could cope with. I couldn't argue with that, in fact in my own mind I was prepared to go further. Not only was Masters as good as dead. So was I, if these guys caught on to us.

'I'll try,' I muttered, and I meant it.

'What's all that whispering out there?'

A familiar bellow from the room Bentley had just left told me Masters was very much alive at the moment. Bentley and I went in to him.

'You're ahead of schedule, Scott boy,' roared the Senator. 'Want to get to it, eh? Well you ain't more anxious'n I am Scotty. Want a little snifter 'fore we go?'

It was one way to introduce a little delay. Might give Bentley and me another couple of minutes to talk sense into this bull-head.

'Thanks. Scotch'll be fine.'

While Bentley got the drink, Masters looked at me appraisingly.

'Been trying to think why you got those duds on, Scott. Worked it out, now. You figure we go in some cheap joint looking like we got it, somebody is liable to try to take it away from us, eh?'

I nodded, wondering why he felt it necessary to talk like some Bowery bum.

'You got it, Ed. Place like Irish Mollies, why those guys'd steal the false teeth right out of your mouth and leave the plate behind.'

'And leave the plate behind,' he guffawed. 'Oh say, I like that.'

He slapped at his knee to give emphasis to the words. But as I'd noted the night before, his changes of mood were mercurial.

'Did you tell 'em?' he enquired suspiciously.

'Did I tell who what?'

'Don't act innocent with me, boy. You trying to tell me the cops haven't grilled you about tonight? Cause if you are, I'm just going to have to say you're a liar.'

'No,' I admitted. 'That's not what I'm saying. Yes, they had a talk to me.'

'I'll bet. Did you spill?'

'No. I told them the best thing I could think of. Said you had some place already in mind, and you wouldn't even tell me until tonight.'

'That was using your head, Scott,' he

149

nodded. 'Why didn't you tell 'em?'

'What kind of a question is that?' I countered. 'You told me to keep it to myself.'

He held up a large paw.

'Oh sure, I told you. But that was last night. Didn't these guys make a big scene out of it. Duty to your country, how would you feel if anything happened to a big public figure. All that jive?'

'Yes. Yes they played that angle into the ground.'

'So why didn't you tell 'em?' he insisted. 'You're an American citizen aren't you. Sense of civic responsibility. Why didn't you tell 'em?'

I weighed my answer carefully while I took a swallow at the drink Bentley pushed into my hand. Looking at Masters I jerked a thumb in the direction of his worried assistant.

'He stopped me. He told me if I let this out of the bag you'd take off on your own, and then you'd be a sitting duck. He thought it was better for you to have at least one friend than be out there on your own.'

I nodded towards the windows. Masters looked at me queerly.

'I don't get it. Mind you, don't make any mistake. I think Ray and these other people make a lot out of nothing. I don't believe there's anything in all this. But you obviously do. Yet you're willing to go along. Why?'

I was ready for that one too.

'When you get my bill you'll know why,' I assured him. 'Your life may not mean much to you, but mine is worth a lot to me. In dollars and cents, as you'll see tomorrow.'

He liked it.

'That's the only sensible remark I've heard so far today.' Turning to Bentley he said, 'You hear that, Ray? That makes sense. A guy works on his emotions, that man is suspect in my book. But a guy who says he's doing something because he's getting paid for it, that's the boy to trust.'

'As long as the money lasts,' replied Bentley snidely.

Masters laughed.

'True, Ray, true. But I reckon I got enough tucked away in my sock for one night out even at Scotty's prices, eh?'

I couldn't find one thing about the respected Senator to like. In my book he was a loudmouth, a show-off, and tonight would undoubtedly add some other little details that wouldn't endear him to me. But courage he had. Considering that a few hours before a bullet had whistled past him, it wouldn't have been unreasonable to expect some sign of the experience. If he'd bragged about it even, that I could have understood. But it was evident he'd dismissed the whole thing from his mind.

'I caught the news on the radio tonight,' I announced. 'What about that shooting this afternoon?'

151

'What about it,' shrugged Masters. 'Some cranky fluff-duff who couldn't hit a barn door. You always find a guy like that.'

'What makes you think he was just a crank?' I queried. 'Why couldn't somebody have sent him?'

'Like who? Look Scotty, you gotta let me know my own business. The man was a loner, take my word. No, tell you what. Don't take my word, read your newspapers. If those guys decide to knock somebody off, they knock him off. Read your papers. Think about the people they have bumped off these past fifteen years. Africa, Middle East, Far East. Always top-line politicians. Always top-line killers. They don't miss, these guys. That's not in their book. They decide to kill you, they kill you. That wasn't them this afternoon. Just some bum.'

He dismissed the whole thing airily. I wished I could have felt half as confident. And now it was time. My glass was empty and it didn't look as though I'd get another drink. I set it down on a table.

'You got a car here Scotty?'

'Yes. It's out front.'

'Good. Think I'll find an old sweater myself. Good idea, that.'

He went into a bedroom. I raised an eyebrow at Bentley, who shook his head and put a finger to his lips. Evidently sounds carried too well from where we were. Bentley then made a gun out of his fingers and looked at me enquiringly. I pulled the sweater up from my middle and let him see the blue black of the automatic's butt. He smiled slightly, satisfied.

Then Masters was back in the room. He was shapeless now in a voluminous fisherman's jersey.

'Let's go,' he said tersely. 'Don't wait up, Ray.'

Bentley looked his disapproval but offered no comment. Out in the corridor the two plainclothes men watched impassively as we got in the elevator.

'Why don't you boys take the rest of the night off?' asked Masters. 'Nobody left in there to look after now.'

'Good night sir,' said one of them.

Downstairs in the lobby the others were waiting. Masters waved to them cheerily.

'G'night, boys.'

They looked at me expectantly. I made a face to show I hadn't got anything to tell them, then we were walking out to the car.

Masters got in beside me and settled himself noisily.

'This Irish Mollie's,' he grunted. 'Which way do we head?'

I considered as we rolled away from the sanctified kerb in front of the Skyroof.

'From here it's due east,' I told him. 'Take about twenty minutes.'

He gave another grunt by way of

153

acknowledgment. Then:

'We'll have to get rid of these flatfeet. You can bet they've got this crate of yours on every police radio in London.'

'Probably,' I conceded. 'What do you think we can do about it?'

'We can ditch it, Scotty. Ditch it.' He grinned like a fat kid who'd been raiding the ice-box. 'Did something like it once before. In Cincinatti. You know it?'

'I've been there.'

'Man what a town. I'm telling you that is one hell of a town. Provided you get rid of the police escort, that is. Do we pass any subway stations on a busy street? Any with more than one entrance I mean?'

'We'll be in Regent Street about two minutes from now. That's what you might call busy. There's a station at Piccadilly Circus. That has entrances all over the place.'

'O.K. Let's hit that one, then.'

'You better tell me what we're supposed to do when we get there,' I suggested.

'Easy. You pull up outside one entrance. We make it like hell into the place, dive out the other side, call a cab and we're clear.'

I grinned, then wiped it off as some clown in a small, nippy car suddenly cut in on me from the side.

'You don't know the Circus,' I told Masters. 'That corner is jammed with traffic. If I park outside there the cops'll swarm all over me.'

'Not tonight,' he corrected. 'Have to find you first. Tomorrow, yes. Then you've got troubles with the police. Not tonight. Needless to point out that you just add any fines to your expenses. I'll pay 'em.'

It was certainly a neat idea, put like that. And it could work. The driver in me shrieked at the suggestion of parking anywhere like that, but that was the essence of the scheme. Upper Regent Street was filled with fast-moving traffic, mostly homegoing revellers now at eleven fifteen. As the Circus loomed near I jabbed Masters in the ribs.

'Here we go,' I told him.

I hogged the left hand turning out of Upper Regent Street, and rolled round the corner. Then I braked suddenly. Masters was already moving. He'd spotted the entrance to the subway. I got out the same side. It would have been a pity to spoil the evening by getting my head shoved in by one of the huge red buses which were roaring past on the driving side. Masters was already disappearing down the lighted stairway and it suddenly occurred to me that I might be included among those to be ditched. Whether anyone was following or not I hadn't the time to check, and in any case I would have had no way of knowing in those crowds. Taking the steps two at a time I chased after the politician. At the bottom he looked over his shoulder, saw I was a yard behind him.

'Up those stairs,' I called, pointing.

Without waiting for me to catch him up, he dashed up the Shaftesbury Avenue exit. I was level with him when we hit the street outside the London Pavilion.

'In here.' I propelled him through the glass doors. He didn't argue. While I bought tickets he stood ogling a life-size cut-out of a half-naked brunette who was about to be torn to pieces by a werewolf.

'Say, these monsters really live it up, don't they?'

I muttered something, pulled him away from the werewolf's breakfast and into the dark theatre. The main feature was well into its last screening for the day, and there was no one in the absorbed audience who had eyes for a couple of sweatered figures who walked in at the back of the theatre, down a side aisle, and straight out of an exit.

We walked up into Shaftesbury Avenue and I waved down a passing cab.

'Just drive,' I said to the hackie. 'We haven't decided where to go yet.'

He shrugged, pulled down his flag and moved away. Masters leaned back and chuckled.

'That was smart thinking, about the movie theatre,' he complimented.

'You think we'd be better off to ditch this cab and get another a little further along?' I asked him.

'Nah,' he shook his head. 'Not worth it. It

isn't far enough.'

'It'll take best part of fifteen minutes to get from here to Mollie's,' I contradicted.

'Irish Mollie's?' he snorted. 'You don't imagine I'd go near the place do you? You can bet your sweet life old Ray's got that place so stiff with police you could take your old maiden aunt there without getting her shocked. No, that's not for us, Scott.'

Leaning forward he tapped on the glass, and the driver slid back the partition.

'Frances Street,' he told him.

The back of the driver's head moved up and down to show he understood.

'What's in Frances Street?' I asked.

Masters' eyes glistened and he ran a thick tongue over his lips.

'Place called the Peep-Easy,' he replied. 'You know it? Just opened three days ago.'

I didn't know it, but the name of the place, plus Masters' interest in going told me all I needed to know. Four minutes later we pulled up outside a spaghetti-joint. We got out and Masters paid the driver.

'Well, where is it?' I asked.

Masters pointed across the street. A flight of stone steps with an iron railing descended from the street level. A solitary light bulb stuck out from the wall, giving just enough illumination for us to navigate the steps. At the bottom was a closed door. Tacked on to the peeling paint was a sign 'PEEP-EASY

157

CLUB—MEMBERS ONLY.'

I turned and said to Masters.

'How'd you know where this was?'

'Didn't. Not exactly. Just it was opposite the Italian eat-house in Frances Street.'

I also wanted to know where he'd got his information since the place had only been open three days. But already he was banging on the battered door. A grille shot back at eye-level and a man stared at us.

'Well?'

'Well open up, bud,' Masters said jovially.

'You members?' queried the other.

'Sure, we're members. Certainly,' was the reply.

'Let's see your membership cards.'

Masters dived in his pocket, took out some bills. Peeling off two one-pound notes he shoved them through the hole.

The door opened quietly and we went into a narrow, damp-smelling passage. The watchdog closed the door and had another look at us. We returned the compliment. He was forty, hard, and wearing an expensive powder-blue suit. He was exactly the man I would have expected to find guarding the entrance to a place called the Peep-Easy Club.

'Have to sign the book gents. Rules. You know.'

He winked. It only made him look more sinister.

Masters went to the ruled book which

rested on a narrow shelf attached to the wall. Carefully picking up the pencil which was attached to the book by a string, he wrote something and handed the pencil to me. I moved to the shelf. Masters had written in his large square hand 'S. Laurel—Hollywood.' I wasn't feeling very imaginative I wrote underneath 'O. Hardy—ditto.' Running my eye quickly up the sheet I found that the Peep-Easy Club was higher-toned than I'd imagined. According to the register, tonight's clientele already included Winston Churchill, Noel Coward, Jack Dempsey and Donald Duck.

'Straight ahead, gents,' said the man on the door.

We followed instructions. I was surprised at the size of the place when we got inside. It must have been spread over the basements of three or four of the narrow buildings which made up Frances Street. A long bar took up one wall and it took three barkeeps all their time to keep pace with the thirsty demands of the patrons. Nearly all the hundred or so people in the place were men, with here and there a hard faced woman who hadn't come in to drink. A small dais stood on the far side of the room, and here a three-piece band strove sullenly against the noise of glasses and loud conversation.

'So what are we doing in this lovely place?' I whispered to Masters.

'Patience, Scott, patience,' he tutted. 'Floor

159

show goes on at midnight. Then you'll see.'

I struggled up to the bar to get us a drink. There were very few tables in the club and these were fully booked. Most of the customers had to stand, so they must figure the floor show worth it. They were a mixed crowd, no doubt about that. Suburbanites, some of the racing crowd, one or two sophisticates, a few obvious toughies. Here and there was the inevitable uniform, and at one table was grouped a bunch of sailors who didn't exactly seem to be enjoying the fun. While I waited for the drinks I wondered idly which of this ill-assorted mob was Donald Duck. It took a long time to get served. I got back to where Masters was standing and handed over his glass.

'Tell me something—' I began.

'Anything Scott boy, anything,' he assured me.

'You knew this was where you were coming, right from the beginning. You didn't need me to tell you about it and you certainly didn't need me as a guide or anything. So what am I doing here?'

He looked at me regretfully.

'Scott old man I'm going to have to be level with you. Didn't care for hoodwinking you that way, Scott. I'm asking you to believe that. Normally I'm a plain, straight-speaking man. Don't care for a lot of tricks and stuff.'

'You haven't answered me,' I pointed out.

160

'True. That is true, Scott. Well sir, the truth is er—I had to have you, or somebody like you, to throw those hounds off the scent. You know? Like, whatever programme you might come up with, they would sure as hell find out about it some way or other. They'd either wire the room, or bounce you around till you told them, or get it out of old Ray, or something. Whatever you might suggest I'm prepared to take the odds they would have dug it out somehow. So I let you go ahead. Gave the hounds an interest, something to sniff at, keep em busy. You know? So don't say I didn't need you Scott, boy. It hurts me to have you think that. I may not have needed you for the low-down on the fun around here, but I sure as hell needed you as a decoy.'

Great. That made me feel much better, naturally. Being used like some green kid on his first assignment by this fat, flabby—. No, forget it, I told myself. I've been told what to do and so far I'm doing it. That is the important thing. That's what counts. Not my personal views about this or any other subject. So I even managed to talk to the worthy senator quite civilly for the next few minutes.

He was in the middle of some bawdy story when I realised that the band was no longer playing. Masters broke off what he was saying and looked across at the stand.

'Tell you the rest later,' he said. 'The show's going to start.'

One of the sailors walked by on his way to the bar. He carried the blue stiff-peaked cap under his arm to make sure he didn't lose it. The gold lettering on the front of the cap was only a couple of feet away from my nose. I could make out 'TYVA' and didn't need to be a seafaring man to know what the other letters were, the ones out of sight under his arm. This man was from the *Latyva,* the ship Forrester had told me about. It was a safe bet too that the other four uniformed men at his table came from the same ship. Now I knew we were in trouble. Turning I grabbed Masters by the elbow.

'We're getting out,' I ordered.

He shrugged me away irritably.

'Like hell. I want to see this.'

'Don't argue with me,' I snapped. 'There are five men here from a ship called the *Latyva.* It was due for Helsinki, but it's turned up in the Port of London with some cock and bull story about engine trouble. The coincidence of these guys being where you are is too much for my stomach. We're getting out.'

Masters took me seriously this time. Seriously enough, that is, to give me his whole attention.

'A bunch of sailors turn up to see the hottest show in town, and you think it's sinister?' he said incredulously.

'There's no time for arguments Masters,' I

told him.

'Damn right,' he affirmed. 'No time for any talk at all. I'm watching the show.'

Well, I couldn't drag him out. All I could do was watch and wait. And in the end, lose. I hadn't any illusions about that.

A guy in a green suit with a huge bow tie came out on the platform and adjusted the microphone to suit him. He tried one or two gags, but all he gathered was a deep groan from the audience. They hadn't come to listen to jokes. They'd come for something else. Something they knew was waiting behind the curtains at the side. Finally the comic gave it up, said there would now be four specialty acts, an announcement greeted with rapture, and held up a hand for silence.

'Gentlemen, the Peep-Easy is proud to present that great favourite from the Continent, Fifi La Chatte.'

The sailor had collected his tray of drinks now and was wending his slow way back, among the open-mouthed spectators. He hadn't even glanced in our direction but then, if he knew his business, that would be what I'd expect.

The drummer played a roll and everything went quiet. The lights in the Peep-Easy weren't exactly blinding when they were full on, and now somebody flicked off the few dim ceiling lights and the darkness was total. My hand went inside my sweater and closed over the comforting chill of the butt of the .38.

On stage an overhead green spot played down on to the platform forming a ghostly circle of uncertain light. Into this stepped Fifi La Chatte. Fifi had two big attractions, and she let the audience have both barrels straight away. Masters sucked in his breath noisily. The piano player began to pick out a slow blues, and the great favourite from the Continent started to put the audience on to a slow burn. I've seen a lot of strippers, and La Chatte was up there with the best. If she was merely the opening act, I shuddered to think what act number four might get up to.

Masters was standing slightly in front of me, no more than a bulky outline. I stood there feeling helpless. Anybody could do anything they liked in this midnight hole, and I probably wouldn't even get to see them.

Fifi was beginning to writhe now, and the expectant tension in the club became almost a tangible thing. She leaned back, half out of the green light and suddenly it snapped off. A woman shouted 'What the hell' and people started to jeer and stamp.

Masters muttered some obscenity, which I never got around to answering. All at once I knew they were all around us. Frantically, I clawed at the .38. The first blow caught me on the side of the head and may have saved my life. As I was falling forward into a red agony the second stroke hit me on the right shoulder.

There was a lot of pushing and shoving going on as I nosedived to the ground. I wasn't out, and as I fought for consciousness I could hear a lot of shouting. Masters. They must have killed him by now. I knew I had to get up on my feet and do something. Lights were coming on, and I hadn't any business lying down on the floor that way. Had to get up. I managed to make it as far as my knees, then a strong hand came under my armpit, and I was swaying about on my feet. Once I had things in some focus I looked at the floor all around me.

There was no body stretched out. Maybe they hadn't killed him, I thought with quick thankfulness.

'What 'appened to you mate?'

A tall man in a zip jacket was talking.

'Somebody slugged me,' I said shakily. 'My friend, the man I was with, you see what happened to him?'

He shook his head.

'I did. Least I think so.'

This from a shorter man who looked as if he was sorry he'd spoken.

'Well?' I snapped.

'Can't be sure,' he faltered. 'But there was a whole gang of 'em. Seemed to be pushing some bloke towards the emergency.'

'Emergency?' I queried.

'Yeh. Emergency exit,' he explained. 'Over behind the stage.'

'Hey, wait a minute.'

165

Somebody called after me as I lumbered across the room to the stage. The drummer was leaning against the side wall holding his stomach. His face was as green as Fifi's spotlight. She was watching him expressionlessly.

'Crummy bastards,' he moaned.

'Where's the exit?' I demanded.

He jerked a thumb towards the side curtains, now billowing slightly at the bottom. I pushed past the half-nude stripper and found a steel door standing open. Before going through I pulled out the automatic and slipped off the safety catch. I heard a swift hiss of fear from La Chatte as I slipped cautiously through the door. Half a dozen steps led upwards and then there was a long narrow alleyway, empty as far as I could see. I went up fast and ran along the narrow opening, hugging the wall as best I could. Knowing all the time I made a perfect target against the rectangle of light streaming out from the club door.

Then I heard the shots. Flinging myself down hard on the stone paving, I counted four loud reports. None of the slugs seemed to be coming my way. Raising my head slightly I made sure the alleyway was still clear. Then I got up again, moved forward more slowly. When I was a dozen yards from the end a man suddenly appeared. He seemed to roll round the corner from the joining street. I thought he was drunk, the way his fingers scratched at the wall for support. He was a big man, suddenly and horribly familiar. I ran the last few yards.

'Rourke,' I said tensely. 'Rourke.'

Very slowly he took one hand away from the wall and turned to face me. The light from a nearby street-lamp fell across his face. The heavy features were now greying folds of flesh and he was dying as he turned. The dull eyes were masking his agony and I didn't think he could even see me.

'Rourke,' I repeated. 'It's me, Stevens. Jeremy, remember?'

'Tell me something. Anything.'

'Jer—Jer?'

He sounded drunk, but he wasn't. There were four bullets in his massive hide and a lesser man would have been dead already. Now he was calling out the last piece of reserve, the piece put into him by the years of training, the piece that told him he might have to die, but the job was still to be done. And it was the job that counted.

Now he tried to stand erect, pulling himself by a tremendous effort away from the comforting support of the wall. I could see the blood now, welling from holes punched viciously in the front of his body by searing bullets. A great spasm of agony contorted his face, and when he spoke there was little more than a whisper left in his great frame. I put my head as close to his mouth as I could.

'Battle,' he managed.

'Sure, Rourke,' I said encouragingly. 'There was a battle. You did fine Rourke. Tell me something.'

He shook his head, as though I didn't get it.

'B—' he said. Then 'B—'

That was the last sound he made on this earth. His knees buckled and he pitched heavily forward. I did my best to catch him, let him down easily. But he was a heavy man and I still hadn't recovered from the bang on the head. He hit the ground harder than I'd intended and I felt a quick warm wave of sympathy for him. A stranger almost, and yet one of that family I'd once belonged to, was belonging to again for a few days.

A shout from the other end of the alley told me I hadn't time to hang around. I could see three or four men now hurrying up towards us. Rourke would be taken care of. Now I had to consider myself, and what I had to do. It was no part of my assignment to spend the night in some police station trying to explain what this was all about.

I took off down the side street, tucking the .38 back inside my pants. At the far end I picked up a cruising cab and rode to the nearest subway station. Here I got out, waited till the cab's tail light was a red dot in the distance, then flagged down the next one that came along.

'Where to, guv?'

A good question. I daren't go back to the

Skyroof to contact Bentley. The hotel would be alive with police and they would have a lot of questions for me. My own place was off limits for the same reason. Then I remembered a promise I'd made earlier in the evening. I had somewhere to go after all.

I gave him Pat Richmond's address.

CHAPTER TEN

It was almost one in the morning when I leaned on the bell outside Pat's apartment. The block was smart enough for me to be able to see where a good chunk of her salary went. This was a high-rental address. She opened the door almost immediately, took one look at me and said:

'Come in.'

She was matter of fact and business like, closing the door and inspecting me carefully.

'You look awful,' she informed me. 'Are you all right?'

'I'm OK.'

I went in to the stylish room and parked heavily on a reproduction antique chair.

She'd changed her clothes and was now wearing a shantung blouse tucked into tight green calf-length pants. That was what I noticed later. Right then I just stared at the floor thinking about Rourke. Still she didn't

169

probe.

'There's coffee, if—'

'Love it,' I nodded.

I didn't particularly want coffee. I wanted to be alone. Alone to think about Rourke and Masters, and stare at the floor, and know that for the moment I was out of it. I'd fouled it up in a big way. There was nothing I could have done, either for Rourke or Masters, but that didn't count. Only one thing counted with the family, and that was a successful assignment. As of now I was a black mark in the books, a man not to be relied on, a man who'd fouled it up. I knew the system, knew how it worked. With the family you got no medals, no promotion. You didn't even get a slap on the back. You just did the impossible and it was accepted as routine. No matter how many times you did it, none of it counted to your credit when that other time came. The time you thought about occasionally, thrusting it away in the back of your mind, but always knowing it was there. That was the time you failed to deliver. You didn't think about it because if you did you'd have to live with the fact that once it happened it was long odds you'd wind up like Rourke. If you didn't you might well wish you had, the way I was almost wishing at that moment. And I wasn't through yet. The family might not know what a great showing I'd made. My next job was to tell them.

I could hear Pat making coffee noises in the tiny kitchen.

'Can I use your 'phone, honey?' I called.

She stuck her head in at the door.

'Of course. Go ahead.'

I nodded and dragged myself up out of the chair. Walking across to the open doorwav I said:

'Hope you won't mind.'

Then I pulled the door shut. I just caught the quick hurt that played on her face before the handle clicked. I dialled the Grosvenor number, and the burr-burr seemed to sound longer than usual. Why not, I reflected. The place was probably humming. Then the receiver was lifted.

'Yes.'

'Jeremy,' I announced.

'Hold it.'

I waited while he told whoever he told, and while he switched on his recording equipment or whatever it was he did.

'All right Jeremy,' he came back.

'You know what happened?' I queried.

'We know,' he confirmed.

'You know about Rourke?' I insisted.

'We do.'

He waited for me to say something else. I obliged.

'I balled it,' I heard my voice forcing out the words.

'Nothing else for you now Jeremy,' droned

171

the impersonal voice. 'Keep off the streets. There are people looking for you. Call in again tomorrow morning.'

There was a click and I was holding a dead 'phone.

'Thanks for the interest,' I said savagely. The receiver looked back impassively. I slammed it on to the cradle.

The door to the kitchen opened and Pat peered round.

'Is it all right for me to come in now?'

'Sure.'

I plunked myself down in the chair again, and wished I hadn't. The heavy movement jarred the bruises on my head and shoulder and I winced. Pat noted this as she advanced to place a steaming cup in my hand. It smelled good.

'You're hurt,' she commented.

'It's nothing,' I replied.

She took this as a hint that I didn't want to talk, and she was right.

The coffee was scalding and I quickly set the cup down after an appreciative sip.

Till now my mind had been in a turmoil of rage, frustration and some fear. All that, plus the belt on the head, hadn't done much to speed up my thinking. Now, in the calm security of the apartment I felt myself beginning to unwind a little. With the easing of the tension came a more logical flow of thought. I began to think again of the Peep-

Easy and afterwards, not this time as a kaleidoscope of jagged impressions, but more as a natural sequence of events. There had been altogether five men from the *S.S. Latyva* in the club. For the moment I had to assume they hadn't been there to inspect the prominent charms of Fïfi La Chatte. How they got there in the first place was not my problem now. Whoever had tipped off Masters about the Peep-Easy was the weak link, and I might never know his identity. My problem was with the things I knew. And what I knew was that we were there and so were they. Their first move was to eliminate me. That was understandable, and indeed the only sensible thing to do, Then they grabbed Masters. So far as I knew they didn't kill him. That was the first thing I didn't get, unless Masters himself had been right. He'd said he didn't think the shooting in the Albert Hall was anything but the work of one crank, or at most a bunch of cranks. O.K. then, assuming the intention was never to kill Masters but to snatch him. This they had done, but what then? The *Latyva* was under close surveillance, and they must have known it. If I didn't mistake my man, Forrester would have that dockside knee-deep in security men. A sailor wouldn't be able to smuggle a bottle of rum on board the *Latyva* without Forrester knowing. So exactly how did they propose to hump a large man like Masters? They wouldn't get as far as the dock

173

gates. I wondered briefly how Rourke had come so close to them, but there was no percentage in following that line of thought. Rourke was all through telling anybody anything. He'd been trying to tell me something about the battle, an odd word to choose.

Wait a minute. Maybe not the battle at all. Perhaps he meant *a* battle. For a moment I felt elated, sure I was right. The feeling went as quickly as it had come. Even if I was right, how many battles were there in the history books. A hundred? A thousand?

'Battle of Waterloo,' I muttered.

Waterloo. That was a main line London terminus. Maybe he was trying to tell me they were going to get Masters on to a train and— No. It was ridiculous. The British are well-known for minding their own business, but even they are likely to get curious at the sight of five hefty foreign sailors carrying an unconscious man around.

'1815.'

I'd forgotten Pat was sitting watching me. Now her voice reminded me.

'Huh?'

I didn't know what she'd said.

'1815,' she repeated. 'Battle of Waterloo. That's what you just said, isn't it?'

'Eh, oh sure. Yeah. That's what I said,' I admitted.

'Courtesy of our system of education,' she

informed me. 'Take one defenceless child, fill with historic dates, and beat until they're all absorbed. 1066 and all that.'

'And all what?'

'Don't they teach you Americans anything? 1066 was the year of the Battle of Hastings,' she said huffily.

'Hastings, oh yes I remember.'

Then I did remember. Something, or maybe nothing. My memory wasn't working too well tonight.

'Pat, do you have any maps around?'

'Maps? Not big ones. Just road maps of the South of England. You know, for the car.'

'Exactly what I need. Could I see them?'

'Of course.'

It took her a minute or two to locate the maps. The coffee was cooler now and I downed about half of it. After that I felt that with a cigarette I might live.

'These are all I have.'

She handed over an assortment of highly-coloured maps. I found one headed 'South Coast' and ran my finger along the place names jutting out from the shore line. I quickly found Hastings. Then a closer look at that section produced a smaller place name. Battle. And Battle was where the Freedom Council had a reception centre for refugees. I rubbed a thumb along the side of my nose and pondered. Not that there was much to ponder about. I wasn't doing any good where I was, and at least this would be an attempt to do something.

'You have a car don't you Pat?'

She was studying my antics with the map with curiosity which was only barely concealed. Now she nodded.

'Why, are we going somewhere?'

'No,' I informed her shortly. 'We are not going anywhere. I on the other hand am going out. In your car, if you'll lend it to me.'

Slowly but positively she shook her head.

'Sorry Scott, but no. I've sat here tonight for hours wondering if anything had happened to you. I couldn't do it again. If you want the car you'll have to take me with you.'

I argued with her, but only briefly. Arguments take time and I didn't have any. Masters had less.

Ten minutes later we were heading out of London in her small but powerful saloon. I let her drive. She knew the route for one thing, and for another, if she had to concentrate on the road she wouldn't waste my time with a lot of questions.

All I'd told her was we were heading for a place called Battle and it was somewhere near Hastings. I didn't tell her why, and she didn't ask. Also I didn't say what was going to happen when we got there, because for one thing I didn't know. It would be close to four in the morning when we reached the place, and how we were going to find the camp was something I hadn't figured out yet. But at least I was moving, trying to do something.

It was a bright clear night and the roads were almost deserted. Pat certainly knew how to handle the little car, and once we were clear of the London fringes I was surprised to see the needle on the speedo flickering on the seventy mark. Moonlight played on the lovely face, set now in determined lines as she squeezed every ounce out of the motor. I realised with a slight shock that things between Pat and I had changed, and changed permanently. The perfect secretary bit was out now, and once this other business was over, we'd have to be ordinary people again, and I'd have to think hard about how we stood. But that was later, not now. Now was the endless strip of road that unwound before us, and the minutes that ticked away on the luminous dial. of my strap-watch.

We didn't talk much, just an occasional exchange, mostly about the signboards and the time.

I almost fell asleep a couple of times, so smoothly did Pat handle the car. As I was about to drop off for the third time she suddenly said:

'Four miles.'

I made a mumbling sound which had started out to be 'what did you say?' Pat chuckled.

'Battle is four miles. Didn't you see the signpost?'

'No,' I said guiltily, wide awake now. 'I must have been looking out the other side.'

'Must have been falling asleep, you mean.'

I ignored that, because it was true, and started wondering again just what I was supposed to do now I was here. Then I saw a call box at the roadside.

'Pull up by the box, Pat,' I said.

She swung into the verge and braked.

'I'll just be a minute.'

I got out and opened the door of the booth. There was the directory, secured to the rear wall by a knotted length of twine. Quickly I flicked through the flimsy sheets. The Freedom Council Reception Centre was listed. The address was Old Highway, Battle. All I had to do now was find the road. In daylight I could have asked any passer-by, but at four in the a.m. passers-by tend to be on the rare side. Fuming, I got back in the car.

'What was that all about?' queried Pat. 'You didn't use the telephone.'

Might as well tell her, I reflected. It couldn't make any difference.

'Looking up an address,' I replied. 'Trouble is, now I know it I can't do anything with it. Tell me Pat, what would you do in a strange town if you knew an address and didn't want to ask anyone the way?'

She thought about it.

'I'd go into the nearest bookstall and buy a map of the streets.'

'All right. Now try again, only this time make it four o'clock in the morning.'

She thought some more.

'I'd look outside the town hall, the bus station and the post office,' she decided. 'One or other is almost bound to have a map.'

I cheered up.

'I'm getting to be glad I let you come,' I told her. 'Let's try 'em all.'

It was a post office that finally gave us what we wanted. The Old Highway was about a mile the other side of town. Things were beginning to shape up. In less than five minutes we'd found the turn-off, a rambling country lane with a scramble of bushes forming a hedge either side.

'Doesn't look as if there's anything up there at all,' Pat offered.

'There's something up there all right,' I assured her.

She turned into the narrow track and we rolled between the unkept hedges.

If it hadn't been such a clear night we might have missed the entrance altogether. It was about half-a-mile from the highway, a farm gate with a white board tacked on to it. The legend said we were here. I signalled Pat to pull in, and looked at the five-barred gate. Beyond it a couple of hundred yards I could make out a cluster of buildings. Here and there a light burned. I turned to Pat.

'This is as far as you go, honey. Turn this

thing round and get some road under you. Don't hang around anywhere near here. You say Hastings is not far?'

She shook her head.

'No distance at all.'

'Go there. Maybe there's an all-night café or something. If not just stay in the car and watch the sea. I'll come there as soon as I can.'

I stopped talking because she was wagging her head again.

'This is no time for arguments,' I snapped. 'These guys might kill you. Do as you're told.'

That seemed to carry a bit more weight. Her voice shaking slightly she said:

I'll go as far as the post office where we found the map. I'll wait exactly one hour. If you haven't turned up I'm going to the police.'

Well, what the hell, I thought. If there was anything here, anything in my line, one hour would give me plenty of time. After that, it wouldn't much matter.

'O.K. One hour.'

I watched while she backed the car round, her face frightened. Then she was gone.

CHAPTER ELEVEN

The gate didn't creak too much as I climbed over. For the first time that night I wished the moon wasn't so enthusiastic. There wasn't a tree or a shrub between the gateway and the buildings. Hugging the hedge I walked along until I was opposite the side of a long low building. Here there were no lights and it was my best chance of crossing that moonlit two hundred yards without being seen. Taking a deep breath I stepped out from the comforting shelter of the hedge and walked boldly towards the building. By the time I was halfway across my heart was thumping like a trip-hammer, and it seemed to me anybody within a mile ought to be able to hear it. A couple of sweating minutes later I was standing in the narrow strip of shadow cast by the moon at the side of the building. Maybe Rourke had been right, back at that first talk we had. When was it, three days ago, three years ago? Maybe I wasn't fit for this kind of work any more.

Crouching each time I passed a window I edged along the side of the hut till I reached the end. Then I peeked cautiously round, and saw the rest of the cluster of buildings. There were lights coming from two of the windows, pale yellow rectangles against the strong white light from the moon. Lights meant people, and if my hunch meant anything at all, I had an idea what kind of people. Taking the .38 out from my middle, I eased off the safety catch, thankful for the smooth, oiled movement which made no sound. The nearest of the lighted windows was about twenty yards off, in a small square building which looked as if it could be an office of some kind. One foot at a time, I made my soundless way across the open ground, relieved once more to find myself flattened safely against the wall. Safely? Well, you take things as they come, one piece at a time. Nobody had spotted me so far. For two or three minutes I kept my ear pressed against the wood wall but could detect no sound. Then I poked a careful eye around the frame of the window and peeked into the room. Nothing. It was just an empty room, that seemed to serve as an office of some kind. There was a rough wooden table in the middle with some file-trays on it and a telephone. No people. The light came from a solitary lamp that dangled from the ceiling, and I guessed it was left on because of the telephone. Maybe it was the only 'phone on the camp. Satisfied that there was nobody there, I looked across at the next light. This was in a much larger building, a two-storey deal, which was probably the headquarters of the place. Here again there was only one light, and this was on the ground level.

It was the only remaining sign of life in the whole place. If I drew another blank there I was going to feel pretty foolish, sneaking round a camp full of unarmed, sleeping refugees, waving an automatic. Just the same, my heart started its noisy pumping again as I stepped out into the hard moonlight and edged across towards the light. I did my

182

listening stint again, ear pushed hard against the wall. This time I got something, and went rigid with anticipation as a faint scramble of voices came through. I couldn't make out any words, but there were at least two people talking, possibly three. I gripped tighter on the butt of the .38, as if for reassurance and looked in through the window. The first man I saw was Masters. I could have shouted with relief when I saw him, plonked squarely in a chair sideways to the window. He was conscious, and they seemed not to have hurt him. He was talking angrily to the other people and I could see two from my narrow angle. One was Stavros, who sat dejectedly in a corner. The other was the young man who acted as Stavros' personal assistant, Kulbin. Kulbin was wearing a shiny leather belt with a pistol holder at the side, and he stood in the middle of the room facing the others. Just within my view was a pair of feet, which belonged to someone who seemed to be stretched out on the floor with his head away from me. So I had at least two to deal with in there, Stavros and Kulbin. Feet was probably either unconscious or dead, whoever he might be.

There was a door in the opposite wall, and if I was going in that seemed to be the way. I slipped round the corner of the building and along the side. No more lights. Then one more turn, and I was making my way along the wall towards the door. There was another window between me and the door and I would have given a lot for another look inside from this new angle, to see if there was anybody else around whom I hadn't been in a position to spot the first time. But I didn't dare risk it. If anyone saw me it would spoil my little surprise. Masters was alive and well at that moment but they might have instructions to kill him if the marines landed. I didn't know, and I couldn't take any chances. My whole job was to get Masters out of there in one piece.

Ducking under the window I edged along until I was outside the door. Inside the voices were still droning. I forced my mind away from the prickly feelings of fear which were playing hell with my resolve, hefted the .38 and flung the door wide.

The tableau was exactly as I'd seen it from the opposite window with everyone now on different sides of the room. Like looking at a film negative the wrong way round. Three startled faces flashed towards me. Kulbin's expression changed immediately to anger. Masters beamed with pleasure, and the odd thing was, so did Stavros. The man on the floor was Raymond Bentley, and one glance at the staring eyes told me all I needed to know about his condition.

'Scott boy,' bellowed Masters.

Kulbin and Stavros said 'Stevens' and 'Mr. Stevens' respectively.

'Sorry I took so long Senator,' I said,

keeping my eyes glued on Kulbin. 'Get his gun will you, and don't come between us while you're doing it.'

'Scott boy,' repeated Masters, lumbering up from the chair. 'It will be a pleasure.'

'Mr. Stevens—' began Stavros.

'I'll get to you in a minute,' I told him out of the side of my mouth. 'First I want to be sure who's got all the artillery.'

Masters had reached Kulbin's side now. The one-time freedom worker smiled thinly.

'The person behind you has a weapon, for a beginning Stevens.'

'Don't insult me with an old—'

I started to speak but the sudden blur of movement at my side cut me off. A length of steel tubing smashed across my gun-hand and the .38 dropped from useless fingers. I gave a roar of pain and turned, as Kulbin bent to pick up my gun.

Pat Richmond stood beside me, her face expressionless. Kulbin said:

'Well done Richmond.'

Masters laughed and went back to his chair.

'Don't seem like your night, Scotty.'

'Thanks,' I told him bitterly. 'You're pretty damned calm about it.'

The Senator shrugged and began to unwrap a stick of gum.

'Better this way Scott, believe me. All you got now is a bruise on your wrist. Way things were shaping before, I'd have had to use

185

Kulbin's gun on you. Frankly, it isn't my line of work. I wasn't looking forward to it.'

I couldn't believe my ears.

'I'm not very bright tonight, Ed. Suppose you spell it out for me in three-letter words.'

'Mr. Stevens, you have been tricked. So have I, but neither of us is important,' Stavros butted in. 'The important thing is that this animal—' he jerked a thumb at Masters '—is going behind the Iron Curtain.'

'What?'

It wasn't a very bright remark, but it was the best I could do. Masters chuckled that rich sound he made.

'Well, now you can see we couldn't have a no-account little feller like you fouling up the play, Scotty. This is the major league, you know?'

'I think sir,' Kulbin was deferential, 'Our friend is a little upset by the news.'

'Swine,' spat Stavros.

Kulbin flushed, but made no reply.

I still couldn't work out just what was going on. To Stavros I said:

'What happened to Bentley?'

'They murdered him, Mr. Stevens. It was unnecessary and it was done in cold blood. The gallant assassin who butchered this defenceless man now stands before you.'

The lash of his words had their effect on Kulbin, who swore and made as if to go for Stavros. Masters voice cut in.

'That's enough Kulbin. Let Dimitri have his fun. He's going to have plenty of time to regret plenty of things once we get him across.'

Kulbin stopped, shrugged and nodded.

'Look, I'm just a new boy here,' I reminded them. 'What is this all about? Where did she come into all this?'

I didn't look at Pat, just nodded my head in her direction. If I'd looked at her I'd have certainly tried to strangle her, Kulbin or no Kulbin. And I knew that would be a quick way to get dead.

'The whole exercise has been planned in the most minute detail for a long time, almost a year,' Kulbin informed me. 'From the time your name was first suggested as being of possible use, it was obviously necessary for us to have accurate information about you. Miss Richmond was honoured with the assignment. When she reported that the man Rourke had been to see you, we knew you would not be the entirely innocent scapegoat we had planned for. Miss Richmond was therefore instructed to act accordingly.'

This filtered slowly into my head, while I tried to set it against what had happened.

'I get that part of it now,' I muttered, half to myself. 'If I went to her apartment after you killed Rourke, she would stay with me whatever happened. I came here, she came with me, and that took care of me. But suppose I hadn't tied this place in, suppose I

187

just hadn't known what to do next?'

'Then you would probably have passed a very pleasant night with Miss Richmond,' Kulbin said coolly. 'And you would never have known anything of her part in this.'

Masters laughed again.

'Brother, you missed out on that one. I know what I'd have been doing right now.'

'But supposing I hadn't gone to her apartment?' I went on, ignoring Masters.

'It would have made little difference,' Kulbin assured me. 'There are guards all around here. It was only because you arrived with her that you were not seized when you first came through the gate.'

I shook my head with bewilderment, not all of it assumed. 'I don't see why you wanted me in the first place,' I said. 'You didn't need me for any of this.'

'That is part-right, Scott. We didn't need you specially. Anybody would have done. Fact it turned out to be you is just your dumb fool luck. When you couldn't leave it alone tonight.'

Masters heaved his shoulders expressively, 'Well that was done on your own time boy. Can't blame us for that. You should have stuck with Peaches there. You'd have had a more pleasant night.'

Although I couldn't see Pat Richmond's face I could sense her dislike of Masters. Maybe something there I could use later. If there was going to be any later.

'Just how unpleasant a night is this going to turn into,' I asked him.

'That would really be up to Kulbin here,' he replied.

I looked at my judge.

'Well Kulbin,' I asked quietly.

'I am sorry Stevens,' he sounded as if he could mean it. 'Our arrangements in this country and in the United States also, are already made. They cannot be placed in jeopardy. You understand?'

'So far,' I nodded. 'Get to the part I'm not going to like.'

He inclined his head.

'We shall be leaving this place in—' he checked his watch '—eight minutes. We shall go to the shore. A small boat will take us to a submarine. You will come with us.'

'What for?' I queried. 'I won't be any use to your people—'

He held up a hand for silence.

'Please. I am not finished. My orders are quite clear. I am to deliver the senator and the man Stavros. Those two only. When we arrive there will be those two only. I am sorry.'

He wasn't half as sorry as I was. As though aware of the racing of my mind, Kulbin pointed the .38 at me. He wasn't threatening me particularly, merely reminding me that the thing was still in his hand. I walked across to where Stavros was huddled in his chair.

189

'Mr. Stavros I owe you an apology. I was pretty sore about that workout those friends of yours gave me the other night. When you told me you were just testing me out, I nearly took a swing at you. You said these guys were rough, and brother you were right.'

He smiled wanly.

'It is a pity Mr. Stevens, you did not bring with you tonight the other remarkable lady friend, who was with you on the previous occasion.'

I had to agree with that.

Kulbin was six feet away from me. Every time I moved, he moved, always maintaining that two-yard gap. As far as I knew he was the only one in the room with a gun. There wasn't any real reason why Masters should have one, but even if he did it was out of view. The same went for Pat Richmond. That meant if I could get Kulbin's weapon I'd be holding it before either of them could produce any artillery that might be out of sight. The big 'if' was Kulbin. He never took his eyes off me, and although he might have nothing personal against me I knew what he'd do if he had to. And if I was in any doubt, Bentley's warm corpse provided a clear example.

Suddenly Kulbin turned to Pat.

'Stand in the doorway and wave,' he instructed.

She went and did that. Immediately a car started somewhere.

190

'It is time,' announced Kulbin. 'When the car comes, you Stevens will get in at the back. Lie face down on the floor. You Stavros will lie beside him. If either of you hesitates I shall kill you.'

He said it without menace, made it sound like 'I will get you a chair' or 'I will write to you.' Only it wasn't. It was 'I will kill you,' and he meant it.

A heavy car scrunched to a halt outside.

'All right, outside. You Stevens you go first.'

I led the way out of the room. There was a long black seven-seater parked with the motor running. It looked for all the world like a hearse, and from where I stood that was what it was.

Opening the rear door I crawled in and lay down on the expensive carpeting. Behind me I could feel Stavros doing the same. Soon we were wedged together, our faces only inches apart.

'You any idea how we get out of this?' I whispered.

'No talking,' grated Kulbin. 'Senator, if you will please ride in front with the driver.'

Doors clicked shut, and I felt the sudden shock as somebody stepped on me before sitting in the back seat.

'Keep your heads down and your mouths closed.'

It was little comfort to know that the man on the back seat was Kulbin. The car moved smoothly away, but not so smoothly I didn't bang my head on the back of the front seat.

The moon had disappeared behind cloud now and the floor of the car was totally black. Time meant nothing, and the only reality was the constant manoeuvring to ease one aching bone after another. Finally we stopped.

'Wait here,' ordered Kulbin.

He stepped on me again and got out. As the door opened, the sea-smell came strongly into the car.

'You think we may have a chance if we jump these characters?' I asked Stavros softly.

'Perhaps,' he replied. 'But I do not think Kulbin and his men will be so foolish as to get within our reach, Mr. Stevens.'

That was what I privately thought, too.

'Very well, you may get out now.'

Stavros wriggled away from me, and I followed him.

We were standing on a paved road fifty yards from the gently breaking sea. One thing the blackness in the car had done for me was to sharpen up my vision. The light from the moon was faint now through the watery clouds but after the stygian gloom of the last several minutes, it was almost like flood lighting. As I got out I closed the door of the car, from ingrained habit. At once it rolled away down the road.

Kulbin was about ten feet away talking to two men who seemed to be fishermen judging by their clothes. Masters stood to one side, alone. Of Pat Richmond there was no sign. Evidently her part was finished. Now Kulbin spoke.

'Down to the edge of the water. Stevens you stay close to your freedom-loving friend. These men will shoot you if you make them the least bit suspicious.'

The fishermen, I could now see, were carrying short-barrelled automatic weapons. I gave up any ideas about trying to rush them. Out at sea a light blinked briefly, and straining my eyes towards the spot I could make out a dark shape in the water. Together, Stavros and I began to trudge across the stony sand. We went slowly, partly from the heavy going and partly from a joint reluctance to arrive at our destination. Then I could see it, a rubber collapsible boat almost at the shore line, dark figures paddling at the sides.

Suddenly, a blinding light flashed at me, then another, finally a third. I held a hand to my face to shield my eyes. The whole beach area was illuminated like a theatre stage. Beside me, Stavros too was protecting his eyes from the glare.

'What the hell is this, Kulbin?' demanded Masters angrily.

Kulbin shouted something towards the boat in a guttural foreign language. Then another voice, through a megaphone and in English.

'Put down your weapons and raise your

hands. Senator Masters and you other men, lie down out of the line of fire.'

One of the fishermen spat a few rounds towards the nearest light.

'Hit the dirt,' I shouted, pushing Stavros violently in the back.

As I flung myself painfully at full length on the stones, there was a brief rattle of fire. The fisherman screamed, clawed at the sky and spun round. He was right at the edge of the water and as he fell sprawling a small wave broke whitely over his head.

Masters lay on his stomach a few feet away, blubbering with fear and praying out loud. He was disgusting.

Kulbin came out of a different mould. He dived on his face and crawled rapidly towards where Stavros and I lay. At the same time he shouted to the other fisherman to copy him. In no time they were huddled close to us.

'Stevens,' ordered Kulbin. 'Turn yourself round so you are between me and them.'

'Like hell,' I told him.

He stuck the automatic against the side of my head.

'I have nothing to lose,' he gritted.

I wriggled my feet around till I was lying the way he wanted me. Then he made Stavros crawl round so he and I made a rough triangle, inside which were Kulbin, Masters and the fisherman.

'Lay down your arms,' came the voice over

the megaphone.

Kulbin raised up on to one elbow.

'I have three men here,' he shouted, 'Senator Masters and two other men. If you shoot, they will be the ones to die.'

One of the searchlights suddenly swung away from us and played along the sea. From where I lay I saw it pick up the rubber boat, move past, then glide back to focus the boat and the blackened faces of the half-dozen men who sat motionless in it. Now the megaphone came back into play. I didn't understand the words, nor even recognise the language. But the men in the boat did.

'Your friends are leaving, Kulbin,' I told him.

It was true. The faces turned away and the sailors began paddling their slow way back to the dark outline of the distant submarine. The remaining fisherman shouted, scrambled up and began to run through the water. What happened then shocked me. From the rubber boat a burst of automatic fire ploughed into the fisherman when he was half way towards it. He fell against an incoming wave and was lifted obscenely towards the sky before sinking slowly into the trough of the wave.

Masters could stand no more. Leaping to his feet he screamed:

'Help. Oh help me. Oh Mother of God please, please help me.'

Kulbin jumped up too, the automatic

195

swinging round to cover the fat quivering figure, rushing now into the sea as the fisherman had a minute before. Kulbin's eyes were off me for a moment. Leaping up I flung myself full-length knocking the .38 from his hand. It fell into the wet sand and the impetus of my dive put me within inches of the black metal as I sprawled full length on the waterline. I chuckled, grabbed the gun and jumped up, swinging round toward Kulbin in the same movement. I heard his laugh even before I saw the glint of metal in his hand. I'd forgotten about the other gun, the one inside the leather holster. Before I'd lined up the .38, his hand jumped suddenly with heavy recoil. There was a loud bang and an ounce of metal punched violently into my side. I was finished. The automatic fell from my hand as I began to sink towards the sand. From behind there was another crackle of sub-machine gun fire. It almost cut Kulbin in half, the heavy slugs tearing a horizontal line across his chest. Somewhere, far away, Masters shouted with pain, then I was flat on my face, fingers pressed against the red agony of my side, as the blood pumped steadily between them.

Feet then. Running feet, sharp words of command. Heavy black boots appeared in front of my eyes. I was midway between being awake and unconscious. There were people talking, but I couldn't make out the words. Another violent stab of pain as somebody

196

removed my hand firmly from the wound. A new voice close enough to my ear for me to understand.

'This one's all right. We'll be able to hang him.'

A great surge of relief at the first words. I tried to protest about the last part but all that came out was a mumble. Hands eased me onto something flat then I was moving, a rhythmic jogging that meant a stretcher. The movement stopped, then there was a sliding movement which I guessed was the stretcher being fixed inside an ambulance.

CHAPTER TWELVE

After that I was vague about what happened. I remember coming suddenly awake in a white room where a fair-haired young man stared at me in no friendly fashion. Then another time there was a brilliant light shining over my head and a figure in white was bending over my mid-section doing something. Another time I was shouting, and when I opened my eyes I looked straight into the troubled face of a young girl who was holding my hand and smoothing at my face with something. I smiled at her, but something must have gone wrong with my charm. Next time I came awake the room was in darkness and she wasn't there.

I waited confidently for the comforting haze to drift back over my mind, waited to sink back into that other world where dames held my hand and stroked my face. Nothing happened. Gradually I realised what was going on. There'd be no more half-world for me. I was back in this one permanently, take it or leave it.

I was flat on my back in a tall narrow bed. The room was small so far as I could see. Remembering the hole in my side I probed cautiously around with one hand. Nothing. Not merely no pain, but no sensation at all. That meant they'd isolated the nerves in that section, or whatever it is they do. Pulling one hand free of the bedclothes I felt around for some kind of light switch. All my groping fingers could find was a button, and this I pressed hopefully. No light. Great. Next, I prodded at the side of the bed to see if there was a table. There was, but there was no light on that either. Suddenly I heard footsteps, walking down a corridor. There was a click then the darkness dissolved as a door opened opposite the foot of the bed.

Framed in the lighted doorway was a trim figure in a nurse's blue uniform.

'Mr. Stevens?' whispered a soft female voice.

'That's me, honey,' I croaked.

She stepped inside, closed the door and snapped down a switch. The room was as small as I'd imagined, not much bigger than a cell. Then I remembered what the character on the beach had said, and looked quickly for the window. No bars.

Soft-voice was now standing beside me, a grave-faced lass with a clean, country kind of appearance.

'How are you feeling now, Mr. Stevens?'

'Now?' I queried. 'Have we met before?'

Some of the gravity left her face as a merry twinkle appeared in her eyes.

'Met? Why, Mr. Stevens, we're engaged.'

'Huh?'

'Yes. And you can't wriggle out of it. You asked me to marry you this afternoon in front of two doctors and an assistant matron.'

'Oh, fine.'

'How are you feeling?'

How was I feeling? I didn't know exactly. Worried, curious, weak, thirsty, hungry. What ought to take precedence?

'What time is it?' I asked her.

'It's ten-fifteen. At night,' she added, sensing the next question. 'You've been here more than sixteen hours. It's about time you came round.'

'Can I sit up?' I wanted to know.

If you're very careful, and if you let me help you,' she informed me severely.

I didn't want to argue. It was doubtful whether I'd have made it by myself anyway. Between us we heaved and pulled me into a

199

sitting position. Soft-voice banked up plenty of pillows behind me. The last effects of the dope they'd pumped into me were now gone. I was more or less normal.

'That feel better?'

I flexed my shoulders.

'Great,' I assured her. 'Hey, I feel great. What's your name honey? And don't say it's nurse.'

She hesitated then,

'Well, since we're going to be married I'll tell you. It's Eileen. Eileen Fraser.'

'O.K. Eileen Fraser, go and drum up some grub, will you? I am the hungriest patient you ever had in good old—Hey what is this place, anyway?'

'Mill Road Memorial Hospital.'

'—in the good old Mill Road Memorial Hospital. Say,' I added suspiciously, 'Will you be able to get me anything to eat at this hour of the night? Most of the hospitals I know are kind of strict about hours.'

She nodded.

'And none stricter than this one, I can tell you. But you're a very unusual patient. You can have anything you like, more or less at any time. Visitors all round the clock. I tell you, Mr. Stevens, you're an object of great interest to the whole staff here.'

'Really?' I realised I might have to watch my words. 'What's so special about me?'

'Oh, nothing much,' she scoffed. 'You arrive

here at the crack of dawn with a bullet hole in you. There are soldiers to keep anybody from getting too close to you. Your clothes are soaked in sea-water. You get a private room, with a guard outside the door, and every hour somebody telephones from London to find out how you are. Why Mr. Stevens, we have patients like you by the dozen.'

I digested all that in silence. My new fiancée was obviously bursting at the seams with curiosity, but she'd have to get on with it.

'Well, seeing I'm such a special customer, you wouldn't want me to starve to death, huh?'

'Oh, very well. I didn't think you'd tell me anyway.'

She went out to see about the food. I was relieved to find they'd left my things on the small table, including cigarettes. I lit one with great anticipation. It tasted like a horse-hair blanket and I quickly stubbed it in the metal ash-tray. I had plenty to think about, and lots of questions to ask somebody, in good time. But right then all I could get interested in was what I was going to get to eat, and whether there'd be enough of it.

It was ham and eggs, piled high on the plate. Twenty minutes later I sat stirring at my second cup of coffee, when Eileen came back for the dishes. We had some banter about the food, then she said:

'I couldn't stop them finding out you were conscious. They heard the buzzer when you first pushed it. Are you ready to see them now?'

'Who are "them" exactly?'

'I don't know. Very important, certainly. One of them is a real gentleman, you know, "the sun never sets".'

That had to be Forrester, I imagined.

'O.K. I've had the hearty meal,' I grinned. 'Trot in the executioners.'

She went out and within a couple of minutes the door opened again and two men came in. The first one was a stranger, but the second was Forrester all right.

'My dear chap,' he greeted. 'Delighted to see you looking so fit. This is a colleague of mine.'

If the colleague had a name, it wasn't being bandied around in hospital rooms. He was a sparely-built man of medium height, very military in appearance and bearing.

'Nice of you to spare us a few minutes Stevens, after what you've been through.'

His voice was clipped and military too. I bowed my head.

'There are some chairs over by that wall, gentlemen. Might as well be comfortable.'

They scraped the chairs across and sat at the foot of the bed, where I could look at both of them without having to turn my head. Very considerate, I reflected.

Forrester said to the other man, whom I'd privately christened 'the General'.

'Perhaps I ought to start things off, sir?'

The other nodded, and Forrester turned to me.

'First of all, let's have the whole story about what happened from the time you left the Skyroof Hotel with Senator Masters.'

I told them. Taking advantage of the hospital surroundings, I talked slowly as though not yet quite recovered. What I was really doing was thinking ahead as much as I could. These people knew nothing about my connection with the family, at least not so far as I was aware, and it was no time for me to be giving away that kind of information now. So I went slowly, very slowly indeed when I got to the part about Rourke. Only just in time did I remember I wasn't supposed even to know his name, or whether he was on our side or the other. If they noticed my hesitation at all, they put it down to the after-effects of shock, plus the dope I'd been getting. Forrester went easy on me, pumping in his questions naturally, and drawing out all he wanted to know without making me feel like the number one suspect in a homicide case. When I was finally through, Forrester said:

'I think that about brings us up-to-date sir?'

The General nodded.

'You did very well Stevens, very well indeed. Lucky thing you had that early army training for this kind of work eh? Came in handy, I fancy?'

'Oh yes, it did,' I agreed. 'There were times though, when I wished the training hadn't been so long ago. Man gets fatter than he thinks.'

They both chuckled. Then the General said seriously:

'Want you to know our people appreciate what you did. May as well tell you, when Forrester here first told me about his talk with you the other evening, I was not enthusiastic about letting you carry on. But in the long run I've been proved wrong, and I'm glad.'

'Thank you,' I acknowledged. 'Don't forget though, I wasn't much use at the end. If your boys hadn't been waiting on that beach, I'd be fish bait by now. How'd they ever get there anyway?'

Forrester smiled.

'Well, you must remember you weren't the only one involved in all this. We've been checking on the movements of a number of other people twenty-four hours a day for the past four days. Two of them were tracked down to the refugee reception centre by two independent teams. Kulbin was one, and the other man you wouldn't have known, but he was involved. That army detachment you ran into was only one of three we had alerted in different places. I'm afraid all the others managed to bag was a long cold night out in the fresh air.'

'I see.'

There were so many questions I wanted answered that I was busy trying to sort them into order of importance, when the General coughed busily and began to speak.

'The reason I am here is because I have been instructed to—er—have a chat with you about this business. These are trying times, Stevens. Busy times too, for people like Forrester and myself. This cold war business makes certain there's always plenty for us to do, eh Forrester?'

'Absolutely, sir,' agreed Forrester.

'Now the way you've played your part in all this tells us a good deal about you, about what sort of man you are. So I don't think I shall have much difficulty in getting you to see our point of view.'

He coughed again. I stared at the white sheet folded back in front of me, and waited for the rest of it.

'You've been put to a great deal of trouble, even got yourself shot, and naturally you won't feel that you can forget the whole business ever happened.'

I nodded.

'Naturally.'

'Nevertheless,' he pressed on, 'that is exactly why I am here. To ask you to forget all about it. Neither your government nor my own wants any of this to leak out. Our relations with— with these other people are balanced very delicately at this time. An affair such as this, if it became known, would not help matters at all. Not at all.'

'Let me ask a question,' I almost called him 'General'. 'It's all very fine to come in here asking me to forget the whole thing. That's not an easy matter, but let's suppose for a moment I'm prepared to agree. That won't change a thing. It did happen, that's what's important. What about everybody else involved? Especially what about those "other people" you mentioned? You don't imagine they'll forget about it too, do you? Seems to me you're a little late. The time to have put your proposition was before anything did happen. Any damage that might be done to relations between governments took place on that beach this morning. Nothing you or I can do is going to change it.'

He listened with a half-smile playing round his lips. When I was finished he grinned widely. Forrester was displaying his teeth too.

'Did I say something funny?' I enquired peevishly.

'Not from your point of view Stevens, no,' admitted the General. 'However, I can quite see how this would look to you, so perhaps a little further explanation is in order. It will make things clearer. Do you mind if I smoke, are you up to it?'

'Go ahead.'

I declined one of the short fat cigars and so did Forrester. The General fussed around

206

happily with a small silver cutter which he took from his jacket, and soon a faint yellow haze began to pollute the air. His lungs must be made of leather, I reflected.

'The international game,' he said from behind an acrid cloud, 'Is something for specialists. The game is played on a number of levels, many of them public, some known only to a privileged few. However there is one level where the play is always hidden. Here there are no victories, no defeats. Nobody ever gets a medal, or his name in the newspapers. Just a lot of discomfort, some danger, no praise. It is reserved for professionals. The rules are very strict, and one mistake means the player is. disqualified, if not already dead. This is the level you stumbled into by accident. You should be dead too, and can count yourself extremely fortunate to be sitting up in that bed.'

He paused to take another puff at the cigar. Or it could have been for effect. If it was, he needn't have bothered. He had all my attention.

'Now, to come to this morning's little party. We happened to put one over on them. You could say we won, in a way. Only we don't think of these affairs in terms of winning or losing. Because you see, the game never ends. Tomorrow, or next day perhaps, they will reverse things. Perhaps in Hong Kong or Paris, who knows? Things are happening every day, and always between the professionals. Let us imagine for a moment that our friends had been successful this morning. Then things would have been quite different. Then there would have been a lot of publicity and hoo-hah. Prominent United States Politician Defects and lots of stuff like that. That would have been something positive, and our friends would have made considerable capital out of it. But the fortunate fact remains that they did not pull it off. So what is their position now? They will be perfectly content to forget the whole thing.'

He paused again, probably because he could see the unspoken questions bursting out of my ears.

'I have all that, sure,' I agreed. 'But what about our, or I should say, your position now. Don't you grab the nearest microphone and shout about how you fooled the opposition?'

The General took the cigar from his mouth and shook his head slowly.

'And what would your suggestion be for a headline, if we did? Prominent American Senator Attempts to Change Sides? It would have to be something like that wouldn't it? World-wide publicity that such a prominent man should wish to go over to them? Can you imagine the capital they would make of that in the new democracies in Africa and elsewhere?'

I could, and I admitted I could see his point.

'To give you an idea Stevens, of how far

ahead the thinking is done in matters of this kind, you have only to cast your mind back to this morning.'

I tried to think over what had happened, but couldn't get the point.

'I'm sorry, I don't think I follow you there.'

'Well, you saw what happened to Masters, didn't you?'

'No,' I confessed, 'I didn't. I was hit while he was running into the sea. Last thing I remember he was screaming blue murder.'

Forrester grinned.

'That could have been at almost any point in the proceedings couldn't it? According to our reports the good senator started to scream shortly after the fun started and kept it up most of the way through. His whole performance scarcely came under the heading of heroism under fire, did it?'

'Not what I saw of it,' I affirmed. 'But what did happen to him.'

'They tried to kill him,' said the general simply. 'First, Kulbin, then the party from the submarine. You put a spoke in Kulbin's wheel, so the other chaps had a try, but the target was already in the process of diving into the water when the bullets came. So all that happened was that he was wounded slightly in the left shoulder and arm.'

I rubbed a weary hand over my face.

'And what's going to be the official handout on that?' I queried.

'I'll tell you that in a moment,' replied the general. 'First I expected you to ask why they did it.'

'All right.' Some feeling was beginning to creep back into my side, and I was wishing it hadn't. All around the area where the damage was a throbbing fiery ache was gradually building up. It wasn't easy to keep interested in anything else. 'All right, why did they want to kill their own boy?'

The general coughed his approval.

'I think it's time you said your piece, Forrester.'

'Certainly, sir.'

I couldn't work out the relationship between these two. From Forrester's attitude it was clear he regarded the general as his senior, yet I had a feeling the man wasn't his boss exactly. Probably operated on a higher level but in a different department, or another branch of the same department. I gave Forrester my attention now.

'To understand the last thing they did, we'll have to sketch in some of the early background,' he began. 'You have had your share of witch-hunts in your country, and at different times different people have come to the fore. All these bodies that have been set-up, committees of inquiry and so forth, all have had made available to them the considerable files and records of your various enforcement agencies. Quite natural, of course. The kind of investigations which have taken place over the years rely heavily on a steady supply of reliable and often secret information. Senator Masters began to draw some public attention with his anti-communist activities several years ago. I regret to have to admit to you that neither your people nor ours began to think there was anything odd about the man until a couple of years ago. There was no reason for anybody to think of him as being anything other than he seemed. A recognisable type of politician in your country, a tub-thumping reform man. There are less of them than there were thirty years ago, but the breed is far from extinct. So, as I say, he seemed genuine enough and his campaigns certainly lacked nothing in their enthusiasm. Indeed, on one or two occasions that I am aware of, your own diplomats have asked that Masters ought to be curbed as a temporary measure, whilst some delicate piece of negotiation was in progress.'

That struck a familiar chord.

'Say, I believe I can recall one such time,' I interrupted. 'The Senator went on television and announced that a certain communist-loving ambassador was trying to get him muzzled.'

Forrester inclined his head.

'That was one occasion, certainly. There were others. However I mustn't digress. A little over two years ago, some of your people had an interesting fact brought to them. Somebody who was working in a certain embassy in Washington had got hold of a copy of a list of names. The names were those of small-fry party members in a large city, it doesn't matter which one. It seemed an odd coincidence that the list was almost identical with one which had been supplied only the previous day, to one of Masters' tribunals. A top secret document, I need scarcely emphasise. I said just now this list was almost identical. The difference was that certain names were missing. The Senator's list had ten names, the list from the embassy only six. The timing of the two lists was too close for your CIA people to ignore. They spent a few days on investigating the handling of their own list, but they didn't trace anything untoward. Meanwhile the tribunal was carrying on as normal, public hearings and all the rest of it.'

Forrester broke off his tale suddenly, looked at me and said:

'I say Stevens, you don't look at all well. Would you sooner we left this till some other time?'

I shook my head.

'Uh uh. I've felt better, but I don't get to hear a yarn like this every day. Please go on.'

'Very well. Er—oh yes, the list. Well now, as I was saying the tribunal went on with its investigation. It took a fortnight and then it produced its findings. The six people on the embassy list were all denounced as having communist affiliations or sympathies. The four remaining people were completely exonerated, and thanked publicly for their free and frank co-operation with the committee. That was normal procedure, and but for the fact that the list from the embassy had leaked out in the first place nobody would have seen anything odd about it. But, with the knowledge that these six people had been listed on a highly confidential embassy report two weeks previously, only two explanations were possible. Either the party had decided to sacrifice these six, write them off the books as it were, or the decisions of the tribunal had been pre-judged by somebody connected with it. And of course, that had to mean Masters. He always had ninety per cent. of the say when it came to summing up. With your record, you don't need me to tell you how thorough your people are in a case like this. They dragged out every document connected with every activity Masters had ever engaged in and went to work. Would you mind if I had a glass of water?'

Forrester helped himself from the water-jug that stood on the bedside table. The general was tapping absent-mindedly at the pocket where he hid his cigars.

'Go ahead and smoke if you want to,' I told him. 'It doesn't bother me.'

'Oh. Well, if you're quite certain. Thank

you, I will.'

Forrester swallowed the last of the water, replaced the glass and went back to his chair.

'Well now, I was telling you about the search that was put in train on all the previous Masters committees. The agents working on it hadn't been at it long when a pattern began to emerge. As you know, little of any real significance is ever revealed by these investigating committees, except how publicity-conscious certain committee members are. Usually they make a lot of noise and finish up by naming a few people in public who've been well known to the government in private for a long time. They produce an occasional surprise, reveal somebody who's never been suspected previously, but as I say this is only occasionally. Masters was exceptional at these revelations. He had pulled several important Communists out of hiding. When I say important, let me define the word. I don't say they were important in the party hierarchy. That's something about which none of us can say with certainty. I meant important in a news way. Business men, actors, all kinds of well-known people. The kind of names guaranteed to draw plenty of publicity, and a good press for Masters. One man shot himself, you probably read about it. A woman columnist jumped from a twelve-storey window. That was two years ago and they still haven't repaired her completely. You may recall that one too.'

I nodded.

'Yes, I remember it very well. I don't see where you're heading though. Surely all this only showed how efficiently Masters was doing his job?'

'To a point yes. Until all the circumstances were analysed. Then a different picture emerged. One of the men was in the advanced stages of an incurable disease. He had only a few weeks, months at most, to live. After that, it wouldn't have mattered much what his activities had been. Another case was that of a rocket research scientist. He'd taken to drinking heavily, and had in fact been sacked from his job. As you know, nobody is ever re-engaged on secret work on any security project once the old demon alcohol rears his lovely head. In three of the cases, people who described themselves as reformed communists gave evidence against the suspected parties. First-hand inside evidence you couldn't have bought with money. Now this seemed really unusual. The cases were all in different cities, so it wasn't a case of sour grapes among a few ex-party members in one spot. Your people thought it was an interesting enough situation to merit further enquiry. They enquired, and were soon satisfied that at least some of those penitent do-gooders were as much involved with the party as they had ever been. Is it beginning to take shape?'

I wagged my head, and regretted it.

'I think so. It sounds as though the senator was being employed as kind of a trouble-shooter, not for the government, but for the party. They used him to get rid of people they no longer needed, or who'd got out of line some way or other. Would that be the general idea?'

Forrester smiled.

'As near as one can guess, yes it would. You see, guessing is all we can do. Nobody is ever going to tell us whether we're right or wrong. But I don't think we're very far wrong. It was a beautiful scheme and better still, it worked. The good senator was doing excellent work for the party, cleaning up the ranks and so forth. On the other hand he seemed to be doing sterling work for the America First fraternity, and this made him a great hero-figure for the publicity men to work on. He became gradually the personification of the fight against Communism, and sat on every possible committee that was in any way concerned with that fight.'

'And,' I murmured, 'Knew every move we were going to make in advance. That way he could keep his friends tipped off all along the line. As you said, it was a beautiful scheme.'

'And as I also said,' reminded Forrester, 'It worked. To the average U.S. citizen of today, America means Edward P. Masters.'

It was true. And if Masters had been

successful in his try to get across the English Channel that morning, and turned up a few days later on the other side of the iron curtain, it would have been a bad blow. Press, television and radio had been busy selling Masters to Joe Public these past years. If Masters suddenly decided to change his political odour Joe might not like it, in fact he wouldn't, but just the same a lingering seed of doubt would have been sown in his mind. Everybody had been telling him for years what a wonderful guy this Masters was, and now suddenly the wonderful guy didn't think the old United States was good enough for him. If a guy as wonderful as Masters could think that, dammit there had to be something in it. Joe wouldn't approve of what the senator had done, but he would never forget he'd done it. Never forget that Ed Masters, who hated Communism worse than anybody, had gone over. And of his own free will.

'Well what do you think of it all, Stevens?' barked the general suddenly.

'I think it's a good thing your boys were on time on that beach this morning,' I replied.

He smiled.

'I agree. I may tell you we wouldn't be sitting here so comfortably, Forrester and I, if it had gone wrong. We'd probably have been roasted alive.'

He said it flippantly, but there was no mistaking the relief in his voice.

'Now that I've heard all the background stuff, I still don't see why they tried to kill him this morning,' I said.

The general bit happily at the stubby cigar.

'That's not too hard to explain,' he told me. 'Masters, you see, is unique. He's not one of a host of scientific or political curtain-jumpers. He is Masters, and fortunately there's only one of him. He had to be successful this morning, there'd be no second opportunity for him. We've tried to tell you roughly what would have been the sequel if he'd managed it. Can you now try to see what position he'd be in if he failed?'

'Give me a minute to think about it.'

They sat quietly while I tried to concentrate. Finally I said:

'How's this? Masters would say he was being kidnapped by Kulbin and the others. You'd never know the difference.' Forrester shook his head.

'You're forgetting Stavros. He knew Masters part in it. He'd tell us.'

'Sure. All right, I give up. I guess you'd just arrest him, have him flown back home and tried?'

The general sighed.

'What a nice direct mind you have, Stevens. How simple life would be if we could run our business on these uncomplicated lines. No, I'm afraid it won't do. You're forgetting that chap we were just talking about, the average man over there. If Masters were to go on trial, the resultant damage would be almost as great as if he'd contrived to escape. The difference between trying and succeeding would be a slight one to our average man. The fact would remain, the indisputable fact, that Masters had tried to go. He'd wanted to go, and that would give our friends almost as good a score as if they'd got him out. No, we wouldn't bring Masters to trial, and they would be confident of that before they started.'

I managed a weak grin.

'Sounds to me as if you gentlemen can't win. Masters escapes, you lose. Masters fails to escape, you lose.' Forrester grinned back.

'Sounds like that doesn't it?'

'It isn't really quite that bad,' cut in the general. 'Now we have to consider the point of view of our friends on the beach this morning. You have already said I think, that you wouldn't have recommended Masters on his bravery today?'

'Long time since I saw such a display,' I confirmed.

'Our friends are very interested in a man's courage, both physical and moral. They would have been able to assess Masters in both respects, with some accuracy. They would have an excellent idea of just how long Masters would be able to withstand some of their more—ah—advanced forms of interrogation.'

'Thirty seconds?' I hazarded.

'The estimate of a generous man,' he commented drily. 'Now you must bear in mind that these people never believe, never really believe, that we don't employ similar methods over here if the circumstances warrant it. They would regard it as a perfectly natural thing for us to do, with a traitor like Masters who has so much he could tell us. It's as simple as that. They would expect us to—ah—extract from Masters the invaluable information he unquestionably possesses. Therefore he had to die.'

'But he didn't,' I objected. 'That was sloppy work on somebody's part.'

Removing the clamped cigar from his teeth the general replied:

'It was bad luck. That burst should have cut him in half. But even our friends make miscalculations sometimes. They could scarcely be expected to foresee that the snivelling coward would be starting to fall from sheer fright before they even had a chance to squeeze the trigger.'

I gathered the impression that Masters hadn't made himself a great favourite with the general that day.

'There was another reason, one might also say a sort of—um—consolation prize for our friends. If Masters had been killed, of course we would have had to invent some suitable circumstances for it. We could never openly accuse those responsible. But whatever yarn we concocted to explain his death the inescapable fact would remain that he had died over here, in Europe. There are always people in your country, patriotic citizens as well, who are prepared to be anti-Old World at the drop of a hat. It wouldn't have been a happy incident so far as relations between our two countries are concerned. All around, I think we can count ourselves extremely fortunate. Yes, extremely fortunate.'

'You've been very frank with me, both of you gentlemen. I'd like to thank you,' I told them.

The general waved his cigar.

'Not a bit of it, my boy. Haven't really told you much you couldn't have worked out for yourself in the long run. Anyway it was necessary for you to be fully in the picture so that you could understand the position we are now in.'

'Or more accurately,' put in Forrester, 'The position you are in, Stevens.'

They sat looking at me, waiting for the obvious question. I sighed and said:

'All right. What position am I in?'

A beam from the general.

'You are in a position to be of positive assistance to your great country, by co-operating with us.'

Suspiciously, I enquired exactly what that entailed.

'Nothing,' he assured me. 'Absolutely

nothing. That is what you have to do, that is what you have to tell everybody about this little matter. Nothing.'

I'd known he was going to say that.

'It's all very fine to say that. You haven't got a bullet hole in you.'

'And neither have you,' Forrester informed me. 'You were crossing some rough ground with a steel-pointed shooting-stick. You fell rather clumsily, and the point of the stick stuck in you. The nature of your scar, when you heal, won't contradict that story. Anyway that is what will be entered in the records here.'

I still felt argumentative.

'And what about Pat Richmond, my faithless Girl Friday? How do I explain about her at the office? And while we're talking about her, whatever became of her?'

Forrester fingered at his tie.

'To take your second question first. She has been released. There is nothing with which she can be charged without attracting a lot of undesirable attention. Her usefulness to her friends is ended. Now they know that we are aware of her, shall we say, political leanings, they won't have much further use for her.'

'That's great,' I snorted. 'She nearly got me killed, that dame, and you turn her loose on the streets of London.'

'That is a rather narrow and personal perspective,' returned Forrester evenly. 'There are broader implications to be considered.'

I lay there feeling like a narrow perspective, and hoped one day I'd get a chance to lay hands on the broader implication that was Pat Richmond.

'If I meet her on the street one of these dark nights,' I muttered peevishly, 'I'll give her broad implications. With me she's just an implicated broad.'

Forrester smiled politely.

'With regard to your other question, we feel some obligation to you about the smooth running of your business while you are recuperating from your—er—accident. We have put one of our people into Miss Richmond's post. A thoroughly efficient and reliable person who has done similar work in the past. Please be assured that everything will run as smoothly as ever.'

I nodded feebly.

'All right, I know when I'm licked. It never happened, I dreamed the whole bit. First thing I'm gonna do when I get out of this place is break up my shooting stick. O.K. ?'

'O.K.' agreed Forrester.

The general smiled.

But I wasn't quite finished with them yet.

'You've both been to a lot of trouble to tell me what could have happened if Masters had got away. Also what might have happened if he'd been killed. So far nobody's got around to saying what is going to happen. You don't turn him loose, I imagine. He's nobody's Pat

Richmond.'

Forrester cleared his throat and looked to the general for a reply. The general looked at me carefully before speaking.

'Of course, it is not for me to decide what will be done with the senator. This is entirely a matter for the authorities of your own country. However, I am prepared to hazard a guess as to what might be done here, if one of our leading figures was involved in anything similar. You understand this will be purely guesswork, and has no authority behind it whatever?'

'Certainly.'

'Very well. I would do precisely what you say we shouldn't. I would turn him loose. He's of no further use to our friends. They now realise that we know all about him, and that means he won't be able to do even one small thing that will be of any value to them. They also know that a man doesn't take kindly to attempts on his life, and that Masters will probably never even have any inclination to work for them any more. He's a spent force, Stevens, and everyone knows it. Their people, our people, Masters himself. I would leave him alone, except for advising him what story will be told to the public about the shooting accident. Aside from that, I'd leave him guessing. He'll be in perpetual fear of further attempts on his life, both from his own late collaborators, and from Stavros' people. Because don't forget,

Stavros knows. He won't talk about it, but he won't forget, either. No, I'd say leave the good senator to his own devices. He's no threat to anybody. My personal forecast would be that within a year, two at most, he'll have retired from public life completely.'

'If he isn't dead,' I pointed out.

The general shrugged non-committally. Then he changed the subject. 'I should think you'll be glad to be rid of the lot of us, won't you? Glad to be back to work and forget this nasty business as quickly as possible. I almost envy you, Stevens. Don't you, Forrester?'

The immaculate Forrester agreed and the conversation became more general.

They stayed a while longer chatting, but the real visit was over. I was hooked, they were satisfied. When they finally went I wondered whether I'd ever lay eyes on them again.

CHAPTER THIRTEEN

Ten days later I climbed out of a train at Waterloo Station in London. My side was still slightly stiff, but otherwise I was normal. Crossing to a row of pay-phone booths, I dialled a certain Grosvenor number. There were curious sounds at the other end, so I tried again with the same result. Then I got through to the operator and told her I was having trouble with my number.

'If you will tell me the number sir, I'll try it for you.'

I spelled it out slowly, to be sure there was no mistake.

'Just one moment,' she told me.

There was a pause. I passed the time studying the excited antics of the stout woman in the next booth, and wished I could listen in on the conversation. Then my operator came back.

'I'm sorry sir, that number is not in service. Are you sure you have the right one?'

'Yes, I'm sure,' I confirmed. 'I spoke to somebody there half a dozen times a couple of weeks ago.'

These telephone girls are just naturally polite. She certainly didn't call me a liar, but her tone said she didn't believe me.

'I'm extremely sorry, but the number is certainly not in use now.'

I thanked her and hung up. It wasn't an unfamiliar situation. The family had wanted something done. It had been done, and that ended it. The bit with the discontinued number was their polite little way of letting me know I was no longer required.

Well maybe they didn't need me, but I knew some people who did. I waved a cab out from the waiting rank and told him to head for my office. In the thick afternoon traffic-crawl it took almost twenty minutes to get there. I got out, paid him off and stood admiring the familiar exterior. There was no telling what mess I was going to find inside, but at least out here there was no sign of termites.

The boy in the plum-coloured uniform beamed a wide grin at me.

'Nice to see you back, Mr. Stevens. All better now sir, are we?'

'We are, thanks. Business as usual around here?'

'Oh yes, sir.' He pressed the button, and we rolled upwards. 'In fact, you've been as busy as I can ever remember, this last week or so.'

I grunted something, stepped out and into the main office. Somebody spotted me, and soon they were all clustered round, pumping my hand and being cheerful. I liked it. Especially I liked being welcome somewhere, after the fast goodbye I'd had from the family.

I grinned at familiar faces, said for the tenth time that I was much better now thanks. Then I asked one of the older couriers:

'How's it been going, Tom?'

He smiled complacently.

'Good as ever Mr. Stevens. Have to hand it to you. When we heard about your accident, and then Miss Richmond just eloping like she did without five minutes notice, well, we thought we'd all be unemployed in a week. How did you ever find anybody like Mrs. Varley while you were in a hospital bed?'

I grinned mysteriously. Not that I had much

choice. To me the whole business was a complete mystery, including Mrs. Varley.

'Just luck I guess, Tom. Anyway I gather it's working out, yes?'

A chorus of voices told me what a wonder Mrs. Varley was. I thought it was time I met the lady.

'She's in your office at the moment, putting some papers away,' somebody volunteered.

I nodded my thanks and left them. As I went through the room which had been Pat Richmond's, I couldn't help feeling a faint sense of loss not to see her pretty face and hear her calm greeting. Still, now to meet Mrs. Varley.

The door of my office was open. As I stepped inside I closed it. Mrs. Varley was leaning over my table. The rear view of Mrs. Varley was very acceptable. I tried for the front.

'I'm Scott Stevens,' I said.

'I know.'

She turned round, and she was Mrs. Varley. Last time she'd been Roxanne Baxter. The name made no difference. She was the same casual beauty she'd been that night. I stood there with my mouth opening and closing. Roxanne laughed.

'Well, say hallo or something.'

'Hallo or something,' I obliged.

I was great. This was me, the smooth, nonchalant Stevens. Roxanne smiled mischievously, darkly beautiful in a clinging red woollen dress.

'Aren't you glad to see me, Scott?'

'I don't know,' I confessed. 'I never met any Mrs. Varley before. Last time you were Roxanne Baxter.'

Her eyes mocked at me.

'That was one of my more plebeian outings. Sometimes I'm Lady Somebody, once I was even a countess.'

'How about Mrs. Varley? Is that your real name, and especially the Mrs. part?'

She held up one hand, like somebody taking an oath.

'No, it is not my real name,' she stated. 'And especially the Mrs. part. I liked being Roxanne Baxter. Did you like her?'

'I liked her,' I confirmed. 'Dammit, you ought to know.'

'I know,' she admitted. 'That's why I'm here. I had a message from a mutual friend. According to him, you think I owe you something. I think so too.'

Suddenly I was glad I'd closed the door.

'Well according to my people out there, you've been doing a first-class job here. Is that your assignment?'

She nodded.

'That's part of it. But we don't have part-time, nine in the morning till five at night assignments. When we're given a job we're expected to stick to it. Twenty-four hours a day.'

I chewed on that. It didn't take very long. I was thinking very pleasant things. And the more I looked at her, the more pleasant they became.

'And, just so there's no possibility of a misunderstanding,' I said slowly. 'You are now assigned to me. Right?'

She came and stood very close.

'Right.'

'Did you bring your knock-out drops?' I enquired snidely.

She smiled a slow lazy smile, the red lips curving back over gleaming teeth. Running her hands slowly up the lapels of my jacket, she murmured.

'Why Scott, that was business. This will be pleasure. And I don't think I'll need any drugs to put you out of action. I know a much nicer way.'

She did, too.

We hope you have enjoyed this Large Print book. Other Chivers Press or Thorndike Press Large Print books are available at your library or directly from the publishers.

For more information about current and forthcoming titles, please call or write, without obligation, to:

Chivers Large Print
published by BBC Audiobooks Ltd
St James House, The Square
Lower Bristol Road
Bath BA2 3BH
UK
email: bbcaudiobooks@bbc.co.uk
www.bbcaudiobooks.co.uk

OR

Thorndike Press
295 Kennedy Memorial Drive
Waterville
Maine 04901
USA
www.gale.com/thorndike
www.gale.com/wheeler

All our Large Print titles are designed for easy reading, and all our books are made to last.